Bonnie Greer wa  in
London. She is a   and has
lived in New Yor   of the
Actors Studio Pla   f the Soho
Theatre Company's 1992 Verity Bargate Award for an
original playscript. She is a regular contributor to *Time Out*
magazine. *Hanging by Her Teeth* is her first novel.

'In her debut novel, playwright Greer infuses the oft-told
story of a woman's search for self with a rich African–
American flavor . . .

Greer takes a powerful and refreshingly unusual stand,
rejecting conventional notions of home and roots in favor
of singularity and independence that add a new dimension
to standard conceptions of black heritage and power.'
Liberal Journal

'Bonnie Greer's novel is a first-person narrative by an
American black woman obsessed with the blues and
searching for her estranged father . . . A beautifully
written, moving book.' *Jewish Chronicle*

'Humorous, sexy and always very sharp, *Hanging by Her
Teeth* refuses any comfortable racial essentialism . . .
Greer achieves what many postmodern cultural theorists
attempt but cannot express with anything approaching her
eloquence; how borrowed, mutable and fragile our sense
of ourselves can be, and she does so entertainingly.' *The
Times Literary Supplement*

'Always fresh, honest and often very funny.' *Time Out*

Other 90s titles

Keverne Barrett   *Unsuitable Arrangements*

Neil Bartlett   *Ready to Catch Him Should He Fall*

Suzannah Dunn   *Darker Days Than Usual*

Albyn Leah Hall   *Deliria*

Diane Langford   *Shame About the Street*

James Lansbury   *Korzeniowski*

Eroica Mildmay   *Lucker and Tiffany Peel Out*

Jonathan Neale   *The Laughter of Heroes*

Silvia Sanza   *Alex Wants to Call It Love*

Susan Schmidt   *Winging It*

Mary Scott   *Not in Newbury* and *Nudists May Be Encountered*

Atima Srivastava   *Transmission*

Lynne Tillman   *Absence Makes the Heart*

Colm Tóibín   *The South*
(Winner of the 1991 *Irish Times* Aer Lingus Fiction Prize)

Margaret Wilkinson   *Ocean Avenue*

....

hanging by
her teeth

....

bonnie greer

Library of Congress Catalog Card Number: 93–86124

A catalogue record for this book is available from the British Library on request.

This volume was published with assistance from the Ralph Lewis Award at the University of Sussex.

First published 1994 by Serpent's Tail,
4 Blackstock Mews, London N4 and
180 Varrick Street, New York, NY 10014

Reprinted 1995

Set in 10½/14 pt Goudy by Intype, London
Printed in Great Britain by Cox & Wyman Ltd
of Reading, Berkshire

For my family, for Kerry, and for David

Athens

To Whomever It May Concern,

Somebody said that if Mick Jagger'd had any kind of respect for himself, he would have been dead by his thirtieth birthday.

Let the church say amen.

It's after midnight and I'm in some no-star hotel on a very hot night without mosquito repellent, with a bunch of schoolgirls from London. For some reason the boat that was meant to take us out to Aegina isn't running, so with the help of a hunch-backed dwarf I found directing traffic, we've landed up in Mosquito Heaven.

The girls are from Our Lady Queen of Peace High School in South London, founded by a group of well-meaning nuns who missed their colonial days in Africa and decided to minister among the disadvantaged of Brixton. I recognize this type of white woman. They gaze at you with this look in their eyes which at once tries to enlist you in their fantasy. You know that what *they* see is some kind of bush station with barefoot little girls with dust on their feet. What *you* see is a posse of home-girls bent on total chaos. But hey, it's a living, if that's what you want to call it.

On my first day there I decided to teach a bit of Hamlet, focusing on Gertrude and Ophelia (in homage to my

Women's Collective days). Well, I couldn't get past Gertrude's name. They said she had to be a stupid bitch with a name like that. I have to say after fifteen minutes of 'discussion' I started to see their point. I mean, anybody named Gertrude had to be guilty of something. Think about it. If your mama named you Hamlet and her name was Gertrude, this was a woman for whom tragedy was inevitable.

One of the nuns got the bright idea to organize a trip to West Africa, so that the girls could discover their 'roots.' I don't think she was ready for the response she got from those girls' Caribbean mamas who don't consider Africa *their* roots, thank-you. So we settled on Greece, and I was chosen to be the chaperone, although I don't know why. Maybe it's because I've been here before. I've been everywhere before. As soon as the plane took off, those convent girls turned into ragamuffin heroines: sequinned tops stopping right beneath their boobs, black see-through lingerie, trainers glittering . . .

We stopped traffic, you better believe it, especially at the Port of Piraeus where some of those old sea dogs had their timbers shivered plenty. They must have thought that 'Never on Sunday' had returned and this time it was black, beautiful, fifteen years old, and speaking in a South London accent.

And there I was, a stone overweight, and praying my £50 perm wouldn't sweat back in the heat. I swear, I tried to be *the adult*, but what I wanted to do was jump in that sea and swim out as far as I could. Maybe to Patmos where St John tripped out, or all the way to Africa, or something corny like that.

Yes, so I understand about Mick Jagger. It's called living past your time.

Tomorrow we go to the Acropolis but these girls couldn't care less about it. I mean, I wonder why I'm even here now.

I know why. It's because I made a commitment. I've stopped moving around. I'm rooted. I'm staying put. I've grown up, in my mid-forties. There's this nice Head Teacher from Barbados who's interested in me, I've met his mother (who I swear I heard mutter 'Yankee girl' under her breath when I had my back turned), gone to church with him . . .

And I'm drinking too many glasses of ouzo now. It's good stuff, this ouzo. I haven't had a drink in six months. Drinking after all that time puts you into another dimension. It's like being celibate and then suddenly there it is, you deal with it, and when the time comes, you realize you haven't forgotten a damn thing.

There's a mirror here, too. Most hotel rooms have them. So many mirrors in the world. Who invented glass? The Venetians? The Chinese?

A mirror. Ha-ha-ha. Look at me. I'm coming at it sideways, but the drink is blurring it all. This is a good thing.

This note will rest beside what I know will eventually be an empty bottle. 'It is written,' like Yul Brynner always said in *The Ten Commandments* while he was getting his behind beat. It is written. So if you only speak Greek, all the better. Then you can just ball this note up and throw it in the garbage. I give you permission. Over and out.

I'm lying on the bed, staring up at the shadows on the ceiling. I'm thinking about the past.

It's like a parade, this thing called the past.

Yours sincerely,
Me

the mirror

Athens

She is in the street again. She thinks she hears the blues in this street. This is why she stops and gazes up at the windows shuttered from the sun. But it is not the blues, only the low moan of the hot wind caressing the trees. She must keep moving. She is searching after all for a miracle.

But she has been looking much too long. Miracles never come when you look for them. Nor do signs. No matter what the Bible says.

She imagines old women peering down from between the slats, looking at her, this strange woman, a little drunk, who has stopped in their street.

What are they thinking as they look at her? Can they tell that she is alone, that she would welcome the refuge of a man's flesh, any man who can quell her contradictions on the cool, scratchy sheets of some hotel bed. She is looking for a man whose body she can stroke like the child she never had. A man she can hold in her arms, a man who can nuzzle her breast and between her legs while she remembers days in front of the television after school, watching old movies and dreaming of making love with foreign men in faraway places.

She manages to resume walking by pretending she is on a tightrope, suspended above a silent crowd. Church bells are ringing. Something inside the bells is calling her.

She always responds to church bells. It was the way she'd been raised. But this time it is not just the sound. This sound is not the sound of the self-assured world-without-end of the Catholic bells of her youth. These are ponderous, heavy, dark bells. They sound like human beings talking. People she recognizes. Like Mr Kaminski, who owned the deli on the corner of her block in New York City. He would sound like this if he were a bell.

Mr Kaminski. Why was she thinking of him right now, right at the tail end of a hot Athenian afternoon, one that had featured a climb up the Acropolis only to look down on a city swimming in pollution? A city floating in the sea of its own past. Like her. Why now?

Because Kaminski had told her once that she would have to go far to find what she was looking for. He told her this exact same thing every Thursday after six in the evening when she came to buy her kasha, challa bread, and mushroom-barley soup. He knew, he said, because he was a wanderer, too. That's why he always had the blues playing in his shop.

She finds the bells. They are ringing from a church on a quiet street. Tourists are sitting on benches there resting their feet. Only tourists would be outdoors this time of day, she thinks. The Greeks are too smart. They understand the benefits of shade, the necessity for coolness.

The darkness inside the church washes over her. It was like being beneath her covers when she was a young girl, reading James Baldwin by flashlight and listening to the sound of the distant train on its way downstate to Cairo, and further south to Mississippi and beyond.

In those days she thought her father would jump off one of those distant trains, make his way down their quiet sub-urban street and at last stand outside her window. There she would look down into his eyes. There she would see her miracle. Just like in the story-books she loved.

He would come inside her bedroom soon after, and she would dig out the broken mirror from its hiding place. Her father would put the pieces back together again as easily as it had once been broken. He would hand it back to her, she would look, the miracle confirmed. She would once again see her face.

The face he took away.

For a time, she gave up on ever finding it. After all, fairy-tales only happened in episodes of the *Mickey Mouse Club*, not on the South Side of Chicago.

Miracles were for saints.

She is inside the church now. There is an icon hidden amidst the incense smoke. It is a black Virgin. Her face is flat, her eyes large and still. The Holy Child is like her, too. The icon must have been waiting hundreds of years for her to arrive. She just knows it.

She places her face as close to the glass as possible. She turns it from side to side so that she can catch her reflection in the dancing light of the votive candles. And for a moment . . .

Has the miracle happened? After all these years, now, in this place, on an alien continent, here? Maybe it's because Greece is so close to Africa . . . or that black Virgins are miraculous, much more powerful than white Virgins.

She can feel the other people in the church whispering, and staring at her. Or is it just her American-induced paranoia? Can't they rejoice at what is happening, at this true gift of a miracle from the black 'Theotokos' in their midst? Or are they afraid of blackness, hers, and the mother of God's?

She looks again. No. She is mistaken. The miracle has not happened. That is not her face, but other faces. Them. The old women of her youth, The Sisters of the Tabernacle of Radiant Energy, white-gloved and flower-hatted, swaying and rocking, their silver-trumpet voices storming Heaven itself: 'No, no, no! I say no, no, no, no! Don't need it. No! Don't want it. No! 'Cause Jesus, sweet Jesus, Jesus Lord is the only man for me.'

And those other sisters, too. The nuns. Long, black nuns with tall, white candles. How she would gaze in rapture at their snow white wimples, at their Bride-of-Christ gold bands radiating against their dark flesh, their faces filled with the serenity she prayed for.

She so longed then to live in their world of silent corridors and prayers in the dark, in their world of order and knowingness, and surrender. She wanted then to be consumed like St Teresa of Avila, lost in a continuous orgasm of the spirit, the flesh tamed. No more wandering. No more searching.

Those nuns, descendants of slaves, too, had found a measure of peace in this world. She prayed she would, too.

But there was no peace, not even now, not even in the icon of this 'woman born without sin.'

Outside the air is cooler. She will go and have a drink in one of the tavernas. A man will eventually come. She may resemble that icon in church, but she certainly wasn't born without sin.

In the meantime, she'd just keep moving. Maybe her miracle would catch up with her.

Voices . . . 'who sitteth at the right Hand of the Father, and will come again to judge the living and the dead . . .'

The drink is making her hear too much, see too much, think too much, remember too much. Remember things like that angel-hair-thin bit of flesh curling from her wrist where she slit it one sunny afternoon. The whiteness of it emerging from her blackness snapped her back to her senses.

'*Introibo ad altare Dei . . .*'

She looks down her body. Her breasts, once so high and close to one another, now sag low to her chest, so low she can put her flat hand between them.

Their present condition would have disappointed her high-school basketball coach, 'the bull-dyke,' the other girls called her. She was a big, Polish woman with pale eyes and red hair, who could play Chopin and Duke Ellington with equal facility.

Every Friday after practice, they met at a diner on the Illinois/Indiana state border where they ate cheeseburgers. Then they would drive to a deserted spot where the coach would stretch her across the back seat and suck her breasts and whisper to her in Polish.

Now those breasts were as flat as a pancake. The price of burning her bra for ten years. The price of being a part of The Women's Collective. The price of being a part of The Black Women's Collective. The price of being a part of the Black Lesbians' Collective.

She had belonged to them all at one time. Why not? Now her breasts were paying the price.

Somebody's singing the blues somewhere. It's a man's voice. He could be right next to her for all she knows. An empty vodka bottle is staring at her. She's pretty sure she's the one who emptied it. The sounds of the cars outside don't sound like American cars. The air doesn't seem like American air. That voice is not an American voice.

She sucks her stomach in. She was taught to do that in school. A woman always had to have a flat tummy, unless, of course, she was pregnant. But even when she had been pregnant she did her tummy exercises. She always tried to do what was expected.

How long has she been here? Her watch seems to have been flung across the room. It lies like a metallic snake, its band twisted around the face.

She tries to see it, but each time she focuses her eyes, her head feels like half-time at a small-town college football game complete with pink-cheeked cheerleaders with blinding white teeth, flashing their panties to the dads in the stands.

She can recall standing on a bridge with two young men, the Bobbsey Twins she called them. One was black and the other white. They were very beautiful and very young. She thought they might be lovers. She thought it might be beautiful watching them make love. Maybe she had even seen them make love when she came to sometime during the night. She thought she saw them kneeling in the darkness, stroking one another, whispering things she could not hear. Or perhaps it had been her own desire made flesh for one split second somewhere in her brain.

She can still hear them now, asking her about America, about New York. Especially New York.

What could she say about any of it except that it had been time for her to get out of the country before it all turned back into Atlantis. She had been very careful in what she told them. That was a reflex. You never know. They could have been MI5, or the FBI, or the CIA. She couldn't help it if she had a past that would interest them.

Anyway, it had all been a series of coincidences. Every bit of it.

For instance, she once had a friend who knew someone who had offered a room to Angela Davis as a safe haven. Angela never showed, but the friend went on to write a book about it and toured the country doing talk-shows on radio stations during drive-time. She was mentioned in the book. It wasn't her fault.

Once she donated some money after a rock concert, where she even danced topless on the shoulders of her old pediatrician. The money eventually went towards leaflets for the 'Days of Rage' when the Weathermen smashed up downtown Chicago. It wasn't her fault.

Another time she gave breakfast to school children as part of the Black Panthers' breakfast programme, but that was only because she wanted to get next to one of them, a tall man whose skin was the colour of midnight and who wore his green Army fatigue jacket like no one else she had ever seen.

It hung from shoulders built like a fortress, and when he wore his tight jeans . . . There were many mornings when she barely missed scalding some poor deprived child with instant grits while she watched him walk.

She marched with King too, but really because she longed to be one of the girls he'd choose to spend an evening with after a hard day dodging power hoses and police batons. She knew the rumours, too.

She often watched Malcolm X on late-night television, armed with a briefcase stuffed with papers and statistics, always prepared in case someone tripped him up. She liked his mind. It was searching, refining. She never took anything he said seriously. She just loved the way he said it. Plus he photographed beautifully.

Some of the things she'd done had to have been observed by someone, someone like Co-Intellpro, the country's intelligence arm, the ones who went to *Hair* dressed in ill-fitting jeans with shirts buttoned up to their neck to take photos of subversives. The subversives were considered to be the ones who chanted during the anti-war demos, 'Pull out LBJ, like your daddy should have done!'

She did that, too, the anti-war marches, because it was a welcome relief from what she considered the bourgeois nightmare of black suburbia.

And who didn't dream of the FOI, The Fruit Of Islam, the elite shock troops of Elijah Muhammed's Black Muslims. She bought *Muhammed Speaks* every week just to watch them, tall, rigid, impeccably dressed in their funeral directors' suits and tiny bow-ties. That tiny bow-tie was the secret of their sex appeal. It was so out that it was in.

That's what she thought then anyway.

She had even said this once years later at a dinner party held in honor of some pillar of the black community. She had had lots of vodka by then. Everyone remarked on it, mainly because they knew her mother, a preacher of high regard and some standing in the community.

Well, she had taken her mother into account, but she had also taken into account that that august gathering was debating the merits of rioting in the street. They bored her. They were laced-up, buttoned-up, and acted as if what had been going on in Watts, Detroit, and elsewhere had had nothing to do with them at all.

They were the same type of people as the ones in the neighborhood she had grown up in who wore Native American costumes at Halloween and dressed up as 'Sheena of the Jungle,' and other assorted myths for the annual summer block party.

They were the ones who believed that NAACP stood not for the National Association for the Advancement of Colored People, but for the National American Alliance of Certain People – them.

She was convinced that someone at that particular party had the ear of the FBI.

Another coincidence. She just happened to be in the Hilton Hotel during that hot evening in August of '68 when the tear-gas wafted up the elevator shaft while she and a campaign worker were wrapped around one another on the other side of the door.

She stuck a blue and white 'Vote McCarthy' peace-and-love daisy on his naked pink backside. She wanted to cover him completely with them, and he was ready, too, when the riot police exploded off the elevators and accused everyone on her floor of throwing excrement down on the police below.

She caught one of them, the sole black cop, watching her with complete hatred and disgust as she tried to find her clothing. He never took his eyes off her.

She always remembered that policeman's eyes because at the time she thought them the most beautiful she had ever seen.

She wants to tell all of this to the Bobbsey Twins she met on the bridge, but you never knew who they might be, who they might tell, and she was a woman alone, travelling alone. Alone.

There is no one here but her, alone, in this room with its

bright colors, its bowl of old fruit, her naked body . . . and the mirror.

She emerges from the toilet and sees the mirror straight ahead. Everything around her seems to be moving in slow motion: the Japanese tourists sucking ice-cream cones dressed in their 'I Love New York' T-shirts; the old Jamaican woman with the blue hairnet talking to herself as she washes out the sinks; the blonde shoving her little boy into one of the stalls, attempting to close the door behind her as she helps him pull down his 'Kiss My Ass I'm Italian' trousers; the Puerto Rican girls with their high-summer beauty, giggling in the doorway as they await their turn; the old woman with the Russian-Jewish accent in the stall next to hers, gossiping to a friend on the other side.

And the mirror straight ahead.

She walks toward it. There is always the possibility that this might be the lucky one, the one in which she will at last see her face. For a brief moment she thinks she catches a glimpse, just the barest slice of forehead coming into view. After all these years . . .

She steps up to the mirror like a nervous bride about to have her veil lifted when a woman shoves her aside, urine running down her legs. The Jamaican cleaning woman sucks her teeth. She mutters, 'ras clat', and 'Yankee' as she hurries behind the woman with a mop.

The good sisters from the Tabernacle of Radiant Energy could come marching through one door and the nuns from every school she's ever attended could come through the other for all she cares. They can hit the mat, rosary beads and 'Good Shepherd' fans flying. Nothing will prevent her from leaving. Nothing will prevent her from looking in this mirror.

Just as she is about to step up to it, a wrinkled, brown hand emerges from beneath the sink. The hand grabs the edge of the wash-basin and pulls itself up out of what looks at first like a bag of rags. A tremendous smell sucks up all the available air. It is a woman. It is as if she is rising from the sulphurous depths. She almost pulls the sink down in the process. She makes a tremendous amount of noise as she rises. The sound echoes through the toilet, drowning out even the pretty Puerto Rican girls.

The bag of rags grabs a bar of soap and begins scribbling on the mirror. The handwriting is as neat as that of her old Palmer Method nun with the wart at the end of her nose and the fastest yard-stick in the West.

'Black. Afro-American. Nigger. Colored. African-American. Negro.' The words sprawl across the surface. There is no chance of anything else being clearly seen in the mirror now. Anything else would be lost in the sea of words.

The bag of rags finishes. She turns to no one in particular and yells in a voice like a blues guitar: 'Yeah. Been called all these here names at one time in my life. Uh-huh. Called myself them names, too! They ain't nothin' but a name. Don't matter what I call myself, still can't get me no taxi in this town!'

She is slowly pulling the waxing tape across Artesia's upper lip. Artesia doesn't want even the illusion of facial hair. That would spoil everything, especially her guise as Wonder Woman, Queen of the American Bicentennial.

Artesia is attempting to adjust her false eyelashes at the same time. 'I hate this damn thing,' she says as she tucks her penis back into the top of her panty-hose. 'Girl, you lucky you don't have to be bothered with all this shit.'

Artesia offers her the last of the flat champagne. She accepts it and drinks faster than she realizes. 'Yeah, but I tell you one thing,' Artesia continues in her Hoosier sing-song, 'beats drivin' a truck full of chickens out of Gary anyday. Hell, I'm really grateful to them chickens. Met my husband drivin' that truck. Huh. Why am I talkin' to you? You don't know a thing about chickens, or truck-drivers, or Gary, Indiana neither. You just a little colored Catholic girl with a preacher for a mama, and an under-used pussy. Lucky fish!'

She was lucky to have met Artesia. By day, Armand Jackson, interstate '10–4 and over' trucker. By night Artesia Wells, panty-hose, skimpy bra, curly black Aretha Franklin wig, blood-red lipstick and all, her beige skin a pinkish orange above the neckline, and rolls of woman-fat above the girdle. Armand was strong and gallant even as Artesia. He treated her like a lady at all times. Especially while tottering down the street on high heels.

'Just remember,' Artesia continues, 'in the end, a pussy is more fun. You can do anything with a pussy. Have as much fun as you want with a pussy. A pussy never sleeps. That's why I'm takin' my ass to Sweden soon as my husband gets out of jail. He's goin' to take care of his black woman. And don't call my husband no dinge queen, neither, 'cause I'm not no bleach queen, no matter what they say. I'm black, and I'm proud. I got my own life to live. Those other bitches say things about me 'cause I got a straight, white man. I know that. See, Artesia don't hang with no faggots. Am I comin' through loud and clear? Come on, take a look at me. Do I look like I'd have a faggot for a husband? Look at all this. Miss Diana Ross of the Brewster Projects, Detroit,

Michigan can't touch it, it's so bad! Come look at me, girl. Look at Artesia.'

She approaches the mirror, her heart pounding. At one time, Artesia was taking instruction in voodoo. With her new powers, she assured her, she could restore her face to her. Artesia took her to a vacant lot where she performed a small ceremony which climaxed in the ritual killing of several chickens from the chicken truck. Then they drank rum and spat it out. The rum was the nice part.

Artesia told her that her face could return when she least expected it. They had killed enough chickens, poured enough rum libation to make it happen.

She looks in the mirror, but only Artesia is reflected there, like a big black baby doll. 'Don't worry, sugah,' Artesia says. 'Let me dress you up. Let me dress you up like a real woman.'

So she allows herself to become Artesia. But there still is no one in the mirror.

The cab that usually takes them to the club is late. Artesia is extremely annoyed having to stand on the corner in the freezing air. She ignores the honking cars, the laughing, pointing boys. She stands facing the Chicago wind, the evil 'hawk', her stockings sagging around her spindly brown legs.

'You want a lift, baby?' a man in a hustler's homburg growls. He pulls alongside in his shocking pink Lincoln Continental with the mink steering wheel and white-wall tyres. There are two other men in the back, their eyes moist, the color of whiskey.

'Naw, baby,' Artesia purrs, even though it's clear she's flattered to death. 'Your party's too hardy.' The men all laugh. The car speeds away, blasting the blues in its wake.

'Sheeet,' Artesia says, hauling up her nylons, 'I ain't suckin' all that jimmy before I do my show. Not puttin' this Revlon back on again for nobody.'

When they arrive at the club, she is ushered to her usual table at the back. A tall albino drag queen in a spangly red dress totters over. She thrusts her hand out like John Wayne. 'Hi. Aw'm Wanda Lust. Aw see you with Artesia a lot. Aw just want you to know you always look nice. Aw like women. Aw have a lot of respect for Kate Millett, Germaine Greer, Gloria Steinem . . . on account of mah ma is a woman . . . aw'd love to impersonate mah ma, but mah jaw's not strong enough.'

Tonight is the Bicentennial Spectacular complete with an Annie-Get-Your-Gun-Act with twenty Ethel Merman impersonators, the usual rosters of Judys, Barbras, Dianas and Chers, and Artesia as herself.

She is offered a hit of amyl nitrate and a watered down drink. She pours the drink down her throat before it waters down further, inhales the popper to give it a kick.

Artesia is given a standing ovation. The amyl nitrate makes Artesia look as if she's melting. A stream of cool air is flowing through the back door. She trips outside, gulping it in.

There, lounging against the brick wall of an old brewery is Morris, a tiny drag queen, his dress over his head. A man in a suit, his tie draped over one shoulder, has his head buried between Morris' legs.

Good old Morris. Saint Morris at one time. Morris had once been the chief altar boy at her school. Morris was the one who cut you dead if you made the wrong response at Mass, or didn't know your catechism letter perfect. She could still see his bright face emerge from the depths of his desk whenever a priest, particularly a handsome, young, white priest, preferably of Central European extraction, entered the room. Before the words, 'Who made you?' left the priest's lips, Morris was on his feet, answering in the automatic fashion that every Catholic child anywhere replies to the first question in the catechism:

'Who made you?'

'God made me.'

'Why did God make you?'

'God made me to know him, love him, and serve him in this world. And to be happy with him in the next.'

There was a time when Morris called her a heretic because her mother was a preacher. He hated what he called the 'choir sissies' who made up the majority of the Mass Choir at her mother's Tabernacle of Radiant Energy. The ones who turned every hymn into the Ring Cycle complete with the Ride of the Valkyries. Not for him. Not Morris. Morris attended two Masses a day, three on Sundays. He knew the name of every Pope since Peter. Morris was going to be a priest and live and die for his people. Morris was going to be the next black saint, canonized even before he died, that's how holy Morris was.

'I figured,' Morris told her once, long after his catechism days were over and he was hustling in the Greyhound Bus station, 'that one of the best ways I could serve God was to make his priests happy, and I've made so many of those girls happy . . .'

Morris is now in a wind-swept alley with a man with blond hair worshipping beneath his raised dress. Yet Morris still has the same face, a face full of that angelic essence which caused the nuns to call him a 'chocolate angel' behind his back.

She strokes his face as she passes him by.

There is a beauty shop across the way. An advertisement extolling the merits of straight hair rests next to another one featuring a primaeval African past in which the inhabitants wear massive Afros and keep them groomed with gallons of hairspray.

She crosses over and stares in the window. She runs her hand across the cold glass. But she cannot see herself. Not there. Not in that cartoon Africa where everyone was royalty and the streets were paved with gold.

No. Only the reflection of the street behind her, and the skimpy trees bending in the bitter Chicago wind.

She is playing with the petticoat underneath her white Communion dress. The dress and petticoat are so white that she is stunned at the way they look next to her skin. She rubs her thigh in wonder. A nun slaps her hand, and pulls the scratchy slip down over her knees. She folds her hands and stands up straight. Winston is watching her. She feels a tingly sensation between her legs which she is sure is at least an occasion for venial sin.

Everyone is here, except her mother who is at home preparing her sermon. Wednesday is sermon day. She knows better than to be underfoot asking questions on sermon day. Today she will have to find out the answer herself.

They walk two-by-two into the church. When she dies and goes to heaven it will be just like this church with its soaring columns, and altar of gold. However, in order to conform to its earthly model, heaven will have to be inhabited first by Italians and Irish, who then move out as the blacks move in. That's the way the world works, after all.

But she can only go to heaven if she keeps her soul white, and this is becoming an increasingly difficult job. Everytime she says or thinks anything at all she can see her soul become riddled with the little black spots called sins.

That's what the nuns said happened.

'Black,' Sister Calixta always hissed as she drew a massive circle on the board and then colored it in. 'Now you don't ever want to have a black soul, 'cause if you die like that, you'll go straight to hell. So you children better get straight, and stop actin' crazy like a bunch of border-line Negroes.'

'What's a border-line Negro?' she had asked her mother on a day other than sermon day. Her mother drew her close. 'I only sent you to those nuns so that you could get the best education you can. There's nothing else a poor Negro mother can do when she wants the best for her child. Anyway, you were baptized because it made your tuition cheaper. We eat fish on Friday so you can be like everybody else. I don't want my child feeling different. I want you to blend in, even though you are special. So don't go crazy, don't get carried away. You're my daughter, not some nun. Besides, you're taking over the Tabernacle some day.'

Yes, she thinks to herself as she walks toward the altar. In some way her question for today has been answered. She will take over the Tabernacle of Radiant Energy some day. Even if she hadn't been lucky enough to die before she reached the Age of Reason like little Michael Bailey stretched out before her on the altar, she is certainly not doomed. Her mother is a preacher, and one day she will be, too.

The procession of children reach the altar. Little Michael Bailey is in his coffin, his brown body swathed in white, his eyes closed. Only four days ago he was throwing spitballs at Father Dombrowski's bald spot. One day later a hit-and-run driver made him into a saint.

Lucky Michael Bailey, she thinks. No more Confession, no

more Stations of the Cross during Lent, no more sliding down in your chair on Friday afternoons during the Tarzan movies while watching the 'natives' who looked like your Uncle Roosevelt or even your own father, go screaming through the jungle with bones in their noses.

Little Michael Bailey's sojourn through this vale of tears was over.

When they reach the coffin, each child is meant to bend over and kiss the dead boy. Her friend Winston keeps pulling on the shiny black braids of a girl called Chita. She wishes she had shiny black braids for Winston to tug. Chita shouts something in Spanish. A nun promptly takes her away. Chita's removal has pushed everyone else up in line. Closer to their dreaded duty.

She arrives at the coffin sooner than she expects. She looks down at Michael's face. 'He's a saint,' someone whispers. Saint Michael Bailey. Could he intercede for her? Could he help her wash away her sins? She's supposed to kiss him. He's the school's very own saint, after all. The second black person she knows of in heaven for sure after Blessed Martin de Porres.

After all she's supposed to thank Michael Bailey for coming down from heaven to go to their school, throw spitballs at their priest, and have his skull crushed outside their church after morning Mass.

The nuns fawn all over him, fussing with him as if he were a sleeping baby instead of a corpse. They stroke his gray cheeks, kiss his hands, tell anecdotes about him. She is expected to kiss him. But she can't. She can't bring herself to kiss him. Old Michael was always tricky. He could be playing possum and jump up and bite her nose.

'I have a cold,' she says suddenly.

Sister Calixta shakes her head. She is also twitching her ring which means she is annoyed. So to avoid Calixta's wrath, she bends down and just as she does so, she catches sight of what appears to be her eye reflected in little Michael's Saint Christopher medal. She glances up for a moment to make sure no one is watching. Then she lowers her head even further to see if she can see her entire face.

Too late. 'What are you doin', girl!' Sister Calixta hisses. 'Move on.'

Her mother always put Sister Calixta's ability to detect mischief down to the fact that the nun was black, too, and from the South. 'She doesn't miss a thing. I can tell,' her mother would always say.

She is lying on her back on the chartreuse mohair rug. Pink Floyd is blasting away. Professor McClaren has already taken her towel off and is busily looking around to see if anyone else at the orgy notices what he is about to do. His blue eyes are eagle-like, much more alert now than in the lecture hall. I guess that's the whole point of this, she thinks, someone has to be watching or it's not any fun. You might as well be at home in your own bed.

The other couples are too busy staring at themselves in the mirror that runs the length of the room to notice anyone else. She wishes she could see herself, but Professor McClaren is so intent on watching himself that he blocks her view.

The woman next to her has stretched her legs open so wide that Professor McClaren takes this as a cue to make an approach. From that the woman's partner takes his cue, and pulls her away from the Professor. The man looks exactly like the picture of Cecil Rhodes that Professor McClaren displayed the other day in Comparative African History 301.

She closes her eyes and turns away when the other man presses his face to hers. McClaren may be her lover, but things have gone far enough.

Before anything else can happen, she jumps up, grabs her towel and walks as casually as she can out of the room. It wouldn't do to be seen running.

A woman with the biggest breasts in the world is being bounced around in a tank near the bar. As she watches this, someone tries to pull her into one of the cubicles.

She escapes and crawls into a deserted room. She presses her face against a mirror. There are mirrors everywhere, but none of them reveal her face. She runs her hand over and over the surface, over and over as if to erase what is happening around her, erase her loneliness, and the other's, too.

She stands on the Bridge of Sighs at dusk. She allows the man to catch full sight of her before the light goes. It amazes her how quickly the sun sets in Venice. It is orange and red and gold. Yet the sun makes the lagoon black. As black as her own skin.

She has stopped walking because she wants the man to catch up with her. She sat next to him on the gondola when they sailed past Santa Maria della Salute. The church looked exactly like the replica on the old wallpaper left behind by the Italian family who lived in her mother's house before she moved in.

The man beside her whispered something she did not understand. She did not respond. How could he know why she was crying? He was quiet for a long time, and just before they alighted at the Piazza, he took her hand and kissed it.

She thought then that he was going to speak some Italian movie nonsense. She glanced at him when he wasn't looking.

She could imagine his face behind a domino, his head hooded, sharp-nosed and hawk-eyed like Dante. Like Beatrice she would lead him across the bridges, to one of the courtyards filled with cats and pigeons existing side-by-side, along the old walls with their ancient balconies and flowers drying in the sun, inside San Marco itself with its Arabic soul, and down onto the cold stone floor to make love while the old women heard Mass.

Later she would drink somewhere hidden with him, and make love in the open air. Since she would never see him again she would tell him everything about her.

About her lost father.

Michigan
1969

She likes Winston's face in the morning. She likes it when he kisses her with his smooth, dark lips. She likes to watch him shave, carefully powdering his face to make sure he does not leave razor bumps on his ebony skin.

'Your father,' he tells her, 'is the only one who can give you back your face.'

She hugs him. She loves his man-smell. Sometimes she doesn't wash because she wants to keep it on her. His smell. The way his armpits smell in the morning, his breath and his hair, too, and how his smell mixes with hers at night when everything is finished and they curl up with one another. He is a man she has known since her childhood. Now he is her lover, her truth-teller.

'You know my father's dead.'

He leads her back to bed.

'Is he?' he asks.

Chicago
1956

The man in the dove-gray suit is here again today. She is not allowed to talk to strangers, but she will talk to him.

Besides, he is not a stranger.

He is her father.

He has come every day for a week to watch her at play. He is tall and black with melancholy eyes. She crosses the street to him.

'Daddy,' she says.

He does not flinch. 'Don't tell your mama I'm here. Do you hear me? How old are you now? Ten?'

'Almost ten. Daddy, you are my daddy. I know you are. Where have you been? When are you coming home?'

'Home? Can't go back there. Got no business there. Look here. You and your mama ought to come to *me*. To *me*. Here. I got somethin' for you.'

He pulls out a shiny foil box. She opens it. It is a mirror with tiny sea shells encircling it. She holds it up to her face, but suddenly it slips from her grasp and shatters. It shatters at her father's feet.

He steps away. He picks up the shards, and the frame and puts them in his pocket. He pulls the hat down deeper over his eyes. As he does so it seems as if the sun itself is going into eclipse. In shading his eyes, he has somehow shaded her own.

'You all ought to come to *me*. Don't tell your mama I was here. Don't tell her nothin'.'

Then he moves into the darkness. Then he is gone.

4 April, 1986
Somewhere over the Atlantic

Dear Father,
My first letter to you in, hell, over twenty years. How time flies when you're having fun.

Today is the eighteenth anniversary of the assassination of Martin Luther King. I have just mentioned this to the young oil executive seated next to me, a very handsome young black man of good education.

I don't know if it's because we're drinking champagne or what, but when I pointed out that today was quite auspicious, he just looked at me. I don't think he knew what I was talking about.

My first thought was that maybe he was too young to know anything about Dr King. But since my young oil executive looks older than five (although you can never tell these days, they're starting them young), I excused the brother and put it all down to the booze.

Something I can relate to.

When he finally pulled himself together, he began to explain to me why Dr King was irrelevant not only to him, but to today's world.

My young oil executive started getting this evangelical gleam in his eye. I let him talk. He ended up by saying: 'Besides, he messed around.'

All this was going on while he was trying to feel me up underneath the skimpy blanket they gave us on this flying Greyhound Bus. You know, the message, not the man. Why are people always looking for messiahs anyway?

I mean, I thought I was being very wise and sober when I pointed all this out to the young oil executive. He ungratefully muttered something about 'that's what all you hippies from the sixties would say.'

A hippie. Yeah, I guess I was, among other things.

When I was a hippie, I once walked behind Abbie Hoffman, who had the best designed raggedy leather jacket I have ever seen. My rags were real.

I don't know what it is now, maybe something they put in the baby food, but kids nowadays have short attention spans. Just when I was trying to bring up one more of my important points about the workings of the world, my young oil executive told me I would look good in one of those 'new' short skirts. He wants to buy me one when we land in Athens. Greece, not Georgia.

In the back of my mind, to tell you the truth, I knew you weren't dead. There were times that I didn't want to admit that to myself, but I knew. Mama finally told me. Mama died a month ago. All those letters! Those letters from Europe . . . Europe of all places. I'm going to look for you there, go to all the towns you've been to and look for you.

Ha-ha-ha, the joke sure was on me. Mama was slick, but you were slicker. Mr Trick-Bag Man. My father.

By the way, this young oil exec. keeps talking about wanting to take me shopping. Probably wants me to try on all the clothes in front of him. Wait until he sees the cellulite. My skin's getting these white spots in places too. I need to lose weight, but to do that I have to stop drinking. Some things are not worth the effort.

The thought of this boy oil tycoon, young enough to be my son, hauling me into some boutique and exposing my over-sized hips to some skinny skirt so he can get off . . . well, I will explain as patiently as I can that a) I wore miniskirts when they first came out, so there's no need to repeat the experience, and b) anyway I'm not staying in Athens long. I'm meeting a boyfriend in Amsterdam who used to be a Black Panther, and is now a member of 'Jews for Jesus,' having converted in the late seventies after being run out of Algiers, etc.

Of course I want to mention that my ex-boyfriend returned to America looking for Eldridge Cleaver and found him a Mormon minister, but that's another story.

Speaking of Amsterdam, you, dearest father, happened to be in Amsterdam yourself for a hot minute. I know this because I saw a letter from you to Mama postmarked Amsterdam. And one from Brussels, and one from Paris, and one from London . . . and the beat goes on. I buried those letters with my mother, your wife.

You killed us both, didn't you Daddy?

Gee, pop, you managed to fit into all the stereotypes there are for black men, and invent a few new ones – you deserted us leaving Mama to fend for us both, yet you managed to keep us emotionally dependent, too, and the new twist . . . you went off to Europe to find yourself! Just like Audrey Hepburn in *Funny Face*!

Don't worry. I was a cliché, too. Harmonica music up (they always played harmonica music in the movies whenever black folks came on), at least I told Mama on her deathbed *that I was going to find you, I promise, Mama!* (Harmonica fade out.) Poor woman didn't give too much of a damn by then because she didn't really know who I was. Strokes can do that to you. But never mind. I'm sure wherever she is, she approves of what I'm doing, and even if she doesn't, I'm doing it anyway. Like always.

Oh well. I think my young oil executive is bored with me. He's now talking to a Dutch girl who it turns out works for Royal Dutch Shell. They're deep into the glories of Brent Crude or something.

There it is down there. The Atlantic Ocean. What that body of water would say if it could talk! It would be a liquid Tower of Babel. So many people have crossed it, willingly and unwillingly. Like me. Like you, sweet Daddy.

I saw a picture of myself when I was five. It was in Mama's things. It was a lovely family picture of you, Mama, and me. Very touching. (Strings up.)

I was hanging over a branch of this huge tree, and you and Mama were kissing underneath. We all looked so happy. I had this look, I can't even explain it now, it was like nothing in this world could frighten me. I knew exactly who I was. Just for a brief moment. I knew then. I knew. I know I knew.

I cannot bury this letter with Mama, so I will flush it down the toilet out into the sea, lost in the world. Oh shit, I'm drunk.

What else is new?

Your daughter,
Lorraine

11 November, 1969

Dear Father,

I'm sleeping with one of my professors at school. The Dean
of the History Department. He voted for McCarthy, and was
in Atlanta for King's funeral. Plus he knows the words to all
of Sly Stone's songs. Real hip, right?

He's told me that he loves me, and that he's going to leave
his wife. I told him to buy me some bell-bottoms instead.
He's introduced me to Cat Stevens, Joni Mitchell, Kris Kris-
tofferson, cunnilingus, and the kingdom of Dahomey, all in
the same session. I said he was hip.

Winston, my boyfriend, may have to go off to Vietnam. I
think he's spending too much time organizing for Biafra. He'll
lose his deferment. I don't want Winston to go off to Vietnam.
Shirline Shaeffer's brother is there, and she hasn't heard from
him. Also, I met this ex-GI who's back to what he calls 'the
world,' I guess he means Chicago, although I don't know how
he could call this town 'the world.' He spent his whole tour
underground in a bunker getting high and fighting the Klu
Klux Klan in the person of a group of redneck farmboys
who'd never been farther than their daddy's cow shed. The
VC just got in the way of everything.

I should be strong and dedicated like the Afro Brothers
and Sisters here on campus who eat, and sleep the Cause. I
envy them. They hate me. They know which way they're
going. Your daughter, she can't even be like the middle-class
ones who have the world sewn up so they can afford to be
'afro-centric' for four years. Or the hippies, or the egg-heads.
Sometimes I am all of them, but most of the time I'm
nothing.

I belong to this group and that group. Sometimes I'm

running from the Black Students' meeting, to the Anti-Vietnam rally, and back again. The black students call me Aunt Thomasina and the white students say I am not doing enough to end the war, (I just found out who Huey Newton was last year. They'd yell 'Free Huey' and the only Huey I knew was Yogi Bear's nephew). And the bourgeois blacks would tell me to get over it and buy a Mustang. (They drive fire-engine red ones blasting 'Say it loud, I'm Black and I'm Proud.')

And that War. That War. You see it everywhere, even when you sit down to eat dinner. There it is, brought to you by Alpo Dog Food. It looks so unreal. Was it like that in your war?

Sometimes I just want to get on a cross-country bus, throw away all my i.d.s and vanish. Vanish like you did.

See, I'm twenty-one today, and I don't want to go on. Great thought to celebrate your birthday with, huh?

Mama gave me a pair of stockings, and some underwear. I don't even think the nuns at my old school wear this mess. It makes me look like Moms Mabley. I'm going to give it to the Missions.

I have to tell you something. You know that I still can't see my face. Sometimes, I don't remember my name. I have to stop and think about it when I'm filling out a form or something. It's scarey. Lana says it's a form of temporary amnesia brought on by old age. Maybe I don't want to know my name. Maybe I don't want to see my face.

I'm in the house alone. Mama's left that box out that she always goes into when she thinks I'm not looking. I still don't have the nerve to ask her to let me see what's in it. Ever since I was a little girl, I always wanted to know what she kept in that box. I always wanted to know.

I have a bottle of wine that Otis Taylor, the boy down the

street who used to have a crush on me, brought by. I'm going to drink some, and then rinse my mouth out with Listerine, before Mama comes back.

I'm still her little girl.

One day I'm going to open that box and see what's inside. Oh, yes. Got to go. The next installment of the war's coming on TV.

Your daughter,
Lorraine

25 November, 1968

Dear Dad,

I'm home from college. It feels really strange sleeping in my old room after being away a year.

Today is Thanksgiving. All Mama's congregation came to eat. This was the big Thanksgiving for the opening of the new Tabernacle.

I had to give a little speech. Everyone kept looking up at me, smiling and pushing me to talk like Mama does. I mean, I didn't say anything important, but they all yelled: 'Preach it! Praise the Lord!' etc.

There was so much food because Mrs Joiner cooked. She cooked a meal for herself, and then one for everyone else. She praised the Lord in between mouthfuls of food. The more I kept talking, the more she kept on eating. I thought she was going to explode.

All these old people, sitting around the table in their best clothes, nodding their heads while I stood up saying nothing.

Because I don't believe anymore.

When I first got to college, I used to go to the bookstore between classes, and read all the travel books. Everything: England, France, Greece, Spain. I just stood there for hours reading and reading until the store closed, and they told me I had to leave.

Then I would take the books with me. I didn't mean to steal them. I just couldn't be separated from them.

On Thanksgiving Day this big white guy walked up to me and said I was under arrest. I have this Afro and wear this Army fatigue jacket all the time with all kinds of stickers and badges. I tried to act bad, but I guess twenty years of convent school doesn't prepare you to be H. Rap Brown.

I had to go to an office in the back of the store. They asked me over and over how many books I had stolen. I didn't know what they meant. They were things I needed to expand my mind and my heart. They liberated me, so I liberated them.

They asked me if I would take a lie-detector test. Well, they didn't exactly ask me. It was take the test or Cook County Jail.

They took me downtown in this old, cramped car. I had to sit between these two jerks discussing the last Bears game. They'd made some kind of bet on who was going to win, and then got into a wrestling match over my lap.

I wondered what it would be like to blow them away. I kept trying to get a look at myself in the mirror doing it, but all I saw was their heads bobbing back and forth.

Mama would have had a fit if she knew. What would I say? I could see her at the police station standing outside my cell, not one expression on her face. And then when the judge asked them what they should do with me, Mama would say, 'throw away the key.' And I'd be happy, because if I was out, I'd be dead.

They took me to this little room and strapped my wrist. This looked like the electric chair to me. Then this man came in, and said we were going to have a little test. He asked me my name. I wasn't telling him. Non-violent resistance. They were trying to test my responses, but I wasn't co-operating. He asked me how I signed my letters. I said, 'your daughter.' I only write to you, and you know my name.

The man said something smart about maybe I didn't know how to write my name. I wanted to tell him to go to hell. That would make that needle jump!

I was asked about the books, whether I took drugs, was I a virgin. I don't know how I got out of there.

But I did. They told me never to come into their store again. I wanted to come back with a bomb.

It was dark when they let me go. I wanted to cry, but I couldn't. The tears just wouldn't come up. I caught a bus to my friend Lana's house. Her parents were at a block club meeting, so Lana and I had the house to ourselves.

We ate the rest of the left-overs and went downstairs to the den to listen to some records. It was good to sit there. Later on, did we talk! We talked about the old days at school. We talked about Judy Faludi at school and how she claimed she got pregnant from a toilet seat. We talked about the Senior Prom, and that's when Lana said that she had always been in love with Winston. My boyfriend. That's all I needed to hear on a day like that.

So I came home for Thanksgiving in a dream. After I said the prayers at supper, Mrs Joiner's brother, Cat-eye, showed up. Unexpected. That made old Mrs Joiner stop stuffing her face.

Cat-eye is a drunk. I see him all the time standing outside the tavern yelling at all the cars that go past. They say something happened to his mind in Korea after Marilyn Monroe showed up once in a mink bikini. They say he had a good mind before that.

Old Cat-eye just sat himself down at the table and ate like it was going out of style. The older men came around the table and talked to him very quietly and nicely until he got up and walked to the door.

Before he left he turned to Mama and said: 'That's why your husband left. That's why your child's goin' to go, too, that's why she got into that white man's car that day when she was hardly fifteen years old. I saw. I see everything. I saw Oswald the day before he took off. Shoot, he ain't dead. I know. Told *me* he was goin'. Didn't tell you. You woke up and one day he was gone. That's because Oswald was a blues-man, and you never did know nothin' about it. But your girl here, she knows. Ask her about it.'

Then everybody looked at me. Well, my heart was in my mouth. But Cat-eye's just a drunk, and nobody pays much attention to what he says. But it was the truth. I do know about the blues.

Everybody tried to get back to normal, because that's how these people are. But it was all over. Mama didn't want me to help wash dishes. She told me to go to my room, and get some sleep. We had Christmas shopping to do tomorrow.

But I can't sleep. I can't. I want to go out now and find Cat-eye. I know he's at the tavern, but I can't go there any more. I can't go there because I might see Claude again, the man I got into the car with. The man who came from far away, from the places I want to see. Auntie Muriel always used to say the older you got the less you knew. She said most people shrivel up inside just like they do outside. She said that the world closes down for most people, or they close it down. It's called settling in. She said human beings aren't supposed to settle in. Human beings are made to roam. Nomads. Not sleep their lives away.

But I'm going to sleep now.

Your daughter,
Lorraine

16 December, 1967

Dear Father,
What makes people afraid? What makes us stop in our tracks and that's it? Auntie Muriel always used to ask that question.

I can't stop thinking about that now that Auntie Muriel has died.

I'm going to play Santa's helper at County Hospital. Mama's really mad because she says that now I'm out of school, I should be in college. But I'm sick of studying. I want to see something.

So I'm a file clerk in a law office. I just file all day and try to keep the lawyers from looking up my miniskirt.

I have inherited Auntie Muriel's old circus costume. The one she wore when she hung by her teeth in Dr Joy's Circus.

Auntie Muriel kept that costume in great condition. It's got sequins all over it. Of course, Mama doesn't know I'm wearing it. She won't know, either. She's too busy raising money for the new Tabernacle anyway.

After you left, Auntie Muriel came to live with us for a while. One day I told her I didn't want to go to school, so she told me I could stay home. She made me a bubble bath. Those were the most beautiful bubbles in the world. She had a pipe, and we just blew bubbles all morning long.

Then she dried me off, and did my hair in a new way. She made braids all over my head, and each braid had a different color ribbon. Then she dressed me in my best Sunday dress. I was only five then but I remembered what she said. She said: 'Always wear your Sunday best.'

We had so much food for breakfast! All the stuff I liked, especially the junk! We watched cartoons. And then she sat me on her lap, and told me about the circus.

When I was that small, I could see everything she said. I could see all the people watching her as she hung by her teeth, twirling around and around, holding those burning torches in her hands. I wanted to do that so much, be so high up that I could see everything, all at one time. Then no one could tell me what to see anymore. Because I could see and be what I wanted.

Sometimes she read her crystal ball. She would look inside and say: 'You will meet a man. He will set you on a journey to a lost treasure. You will find this treasure.'

I miss her. Another thing she said was that being wild was just about the most important thing a colored woman could be. We didn't invent the rules, so we don't have to go by them.

She used to sit in her rocking chair, smoking her pipe. 'Everything you kids doin' now,' she'd say, 'we did in my day. Not the same way, but it was the same things. You marching and protesting. We did that, too. You want to be called black. We wanted to be called Negro with a capital 'N'. You talk about Africa. We had the Black Star Line. We was ready to go back, jack. You got Elijah Muhammed. We had Daddy Grace. It all comes back round again.

'Trouble is, folks keep on repeatin' things. Repeating. Repeating. I hate repeatin'. I know you kids ain't never done these things before. You young folks got to find your own way. We old folks got no business stopping you. But you can't blame us for wondering why you all don't do nothing new. Ain't you learned nothin' from us 'side the mistakes we made? But then, maybe you can't do nothing new because it ain't a new day yet.'

I would bring Lana and some of my other friends around for sweet potato pie and a glass of milk after school. Auntie Muriel told us how sorry she felt for us because we had to wear our navy blue school uniforms most days of the week. Then she would go in her trunk and pull out these dresses, beautiful bright red dresses, and shiny black ones with beads, and green ones, green as the grass, and bright yellow like the sun, all the colors we weren't supposed to wear because dark people aren't supposed to wear bright colors.

We'd put on those dresses, and sit around her feet, and she'd tell us about the chitlin circuit, the TOBA, Theatre Owners' Booking Agency. She always said TOBA stood for 'tough on black asses.'

Everybody was on the TOBA circuit then, Bessie Smith, Ma Rainey, all the women blues singers. Auntie Muriel said that women changed the blues. It was about men's hurt before. But when the women came along, they made the blues big, wide open. They were the biggest stars until the thirties, when Auntie Muriel came along. By then the men had come back, and the women were small again.

To Auntie Muriel, the blues were the most important music of all for black people. It was the basis of everything, of all music sung in America. She said that the blues was not only music, it was a way of being in the world. The blues was about living inside and outside at the same time. It was about being on the open road. It was about seeing things as they really are.

Black people were taken from Africa, but Africa was not taken from them. Africa was where humans began. So an African was a human being, and the blues was human music. It spoke to everybody. If black people lose the blues, they lose their lives.

This is what Auntie Muriel told us.

Auntie Muriel always called herself a blues woman. A blues woman lived life her way. The only law she respected was the one that came from her. The only god she worshipped was the one who spoke to her.

I remembered that when I first went to the County Hospital ward where they keep all the abandoned children, the babies left on bus seats, in garbage cans, on front steps, in phone booths.

Black babies, brown babies, yellow babies, white babies. Why do people scream about babies that aren't even born yet when there are so many babies thrown away and nobody cares? Those babies are the ones we know for sure are alive. We don't have to argue about those.

The ward was full of young babies, but there was not a sound. You know how little babies cry all the time. Not a sound.

I looked in each little face, and all those faces looked right back at me. They looked very old. Those babies knew a whole lot more than I'll ever know. I held one up to the glass. I looked at it. There was that baby, so little with big, old woman's eyes.

I couldn't tell if I was looking at her face or my own.

Your daughter,
Lorraine

13 Oct, 1967

Dear Father,

Mama and I have just come back from comforting Mrs Evans. Her children were run off the road in Mississippi when they were on their way to see their grandmother.

They went over a cliff. All three of them died.

Mrs Evans was so proud of those children. They all had scholarships, even little Carl had one, and he was only six. She bragged about them all the time. And now they're gone just like that. Just like that.

The block is very quiet. You can smell death in the air. It smells like those leaves burning in backyards up and down the street. It smells like everything's going up in smoke. Everything.

Mama wants me to go to college. I just want to get away.

I still go to two churches on Sunday, but I'm just there now. I'm not anywhere anymore. Not after meeting Claude, and seeing Magic Al die.

I've lost my courage. It's just gone away. Gone. I had more courage that summer when I just got into Claude's car. I just got in. I didn't think about the fact that he was a white man, or that somebody could've seen me, or that I could have been dead. I just did it.

Now, I'm like everyone else. I go to school, come home, do my homework, go to church, and that's all. I don't even think I can write to you anymore. I don't think so. I can't express myself anymore.

I saw my history teacher the other day. She is the first teacher I've ever had who wears an Afro. I think she's beautiful. All of us think she's beautiful. Our mothers think she should go and get her hair straightened.

One day, after school, I walked past her room. The door was open and she was just standing there looking out the window. I thought she'd caught some of the girls smoking in the grotto of Our Lady of Lourdes where we always go to smoke anyway.

Miss Washington saw me looking at her. And then she said something very strange. She said: 'When I was young, I wanted to go to Africa. I told everyone about it. I had maps. I made plans. I started studying Twi. I was going. And then, I just didn't see the possibilities anymore. I just couldn't see how I was going to do it. No one tried to stop me. It was just that I couldn't see anymore. *I* couldn't see.'

She walked away from me, like she was sleepwalking. I don't want to end up like her.

Your daughter,
Lorraine

14 September, 1966

Dearest Father,
Back to school. I have a job. I babysit for some members of Mama's congregation. They have a two-year-old. You know the expression 'The Terrible Twos'. This kid Delroy's king of TTTs. He's bad, and I don't mean good. He's got everything

except a sense of humor. What he wants he wants right now and he always gets it. He can sit up all night and talk your head off.

His parents go to Africa every summer, so there's all these statues all over the place. The kid tries to knock them over. He likes to chew the pictures of his father holding up dead lions and stuff like that. His father belongs to a club for people who go to Africa to hunt game. I wonder what those Africans think when they see the 'Negro-American Safari Club.'

I asked Delroy's father what he talked to the Africans about, you know, the ones who carry his guns and his barbecue equipment. That man looked at me like I was crazy. 'You don't talk to them, you pay them.'

Every day I feel like something is going to crash down on me. I think Mama knows I'll never be what she wants me to be.

I can still remember the way it felt riding with Claude. In my heart of hearts I'm not ashamed of what I did.

But as time goes by it becomes harder to remember it all. I sit and stare at pictures of me then, that young girl who had all the courage.

Your daughter,
Lorraine

3 August, 1966

Dear Father,
Now why I write to you in the summer all the time I'll never know. But two letters in a row can't be all bad.

Mama and I are up in the Michigan woods in this cabin

one of the congregation gave her. Mama is scared of the woods because it reminds her of the South and of being lynched. Mama was never lynched and she didn't live in the South, but that doesn't stop her from being scared in the woods. She says it's a race memory.

There are not many people my age up here. Just a lot of retired folks. The 'bourgeoisie' is what Winston calls them. The funny thing is that most of the men are dark-skinned and their wives are real light-skinned. Those women don't even like to go out in the sun. They sit around in big hats and sip drinks and talk about being retired. They don't talk to Mama and me very much. I guess we're too dark.

Last night I went out to watch fireflies. When I was little, I used to catch them and wear them on my ears. And they would twinkle all night. Or sometimes I would put them in jars. But I don't like to capture things anymore.

Mama came and sat next to me on the porch today. She'd been reading the Bible all day. She always has a pretty glow after she's read the Bible. Like she's found out a secret. Something special, something good.

She almost caught me writing to you. I don't want her to see my letters. There are things I just want to say to *you*, things I just want *you* to know. You can't tell your mother everything.

Well anyway, she started telling me about the time when she was a little girl, and her father, who was also a preacher, took her to a huge tabernacle. There were about six hundred worshippers there all dressed in white.

Her daddy marched her straight to the front, to where the choir sang, and announced that Mama was going to be a preacher. Do you know what Mama said? She said no. She was going to be a painter. Then her father just shook her in front of all those people until she gave in and said what he wanted her to say. But she didn't change in her heart. That's just something I know, nobody told me. And then, right before I was born, something happened to her. She never told me what, just that she got a sign. She decided then that he was right after all.

I asked her and asked her what happened. What was the sign? But she said it was too long ago and she couldn't recall.

There is something so pretty about Mama in the moonlight, just when she's sitting there with her hair pulled back, and her white cotton blouse, and those pedal pushers she likes to wear. Yes, I can see Mama a painter. She could have done anything she wanted.

I want to hold Mama. I want to rock her like a baby. But you can't do that to mothers. Especially when you're almost grown.

Your daughter,
Lorraine

31 July, 1966

Dear Father,
Another year. I've started playing this game. I've started pretending that I don't know who I am. Like I have amnesia. It's great. I have this stupid job at the cosmetics counter at Woolworth's and I put different name tags on myself everyday. I put your name on my tag today. But those poor black girls were so busy trying to look like Jean Shrimpton they didn't even see it.

I went over to Lana's last night. Mama doesn't like me to

go because she says that Lana's family are heathens, but they just have two Cadillacs, that's all.

Lana and I saved up our money and then went down to thirty-first Street and bought ourselves Diana Ross wigs.

We dressed up like the Supremes and sang in her mother's bedroom. Her parents have separate bedrooms. That's because her grandparents were sharecroppers and everyone lived in one room. Her father made up his mind that when he could afford it, everybody in his family would have their own room no matter what. So Lana's mother has this pink bedroom with gold fixtures and a deep pink pile rug and lots of expensive perfume, plus a three way mirror. We do the Supremes in that room. (I'm glad Winston can't see me.)

After we did about ten songs, Lana suddenly jumped up and said we should be thinking about all the brothers and sisters in the ghetto and trying to help them instead of pretending to be the Supremes. We ought to be on the open housing marches, or something like that instead of being so bourgeois. I don't know about that. I know I've been deprived because I didn't grow up in the ghetto, but it's not my fault.

I always used to feel funny riding home in the school bus in my nice little white blouse and blue skirt and jacket, while all the kids from public school walked home, calling us all kinds of names and throwing rocks at us and everything. They said we couldn't sing, and they were right because all we knew were Latin hymns and stuff like 'Would You Like to Swing on a Star.' I guess we didn't really know how to dance compared to them, too.

I like to take the bus down to the Planetarium to see the stars and the planets. I like to go outside and sit in that place by the lake where you can see the sun rise. The sun makes the lake look like a sea instead. The sea. All those big ships sailing off. I can see myself on those big ships sailing away, too. Sailing far away. Maybe to Paris. Maybe to London, or Amsterdam. Africa, too.

Singing the blues.

Your daughter,
Lorraine

24 July, 1964

Dear Daddy,
I can't sleep. I lost Magic Al's gold tooth while I was running for a bus. It made me scared when I realized it was gone.

I just keep seeing Magic Al's face. I just keep seeing the way he looked at me before he died.

Winston Smith came to our house yesterday. He was selling candy-bars to raise money for his basketball team.

Winston knows me. That seems strange to say that a boy would know me. But I am him, and he is me. We know that. When I miss my face so much I can't take it anymore, I go to Winston and look deep in his eyes. When I look at his face, I feel that I am looking at mine.

I want to marry him, but I know we never will. We are too close.

I met him when we were little children on our first day at school. I was eleven and he was twelve. There were still lots of white kids there and they didn't like us. After school they would chase us home through the snow. That first day Winston Smith showed me the best place to run, in the tracks left by the trucks. The ground was always flat, so we couldn't fall down. Right after school on the first day, there were the white kids outside and we started running. I ran with Winston down the tracks to a park. There was no one there at all.

That park was completely white, not a footprint, not even from a bird or a squirrel. It looked like a fairyland. It was so still and quiet we didn't want to talk at all.

It started to snow. The flakes were very big and white and soft and they melted on our face. Winston said to me, 'Did you know that Blind Lemon Jefferson the blues man died in a snowstorm?' I didn't even know who Blind Lemon Jefferson was. Then I remembered that you left me some records by Blind Lemon Jefferson, so I acted smart and said 'Yes.' But I didn't know. I didn't know about the blues then. I do now.

We made a snowman. Winston said it might as well be us who messes up this snow, so we did. After we finished, we knocked it down because he said that he didn't want anyone to have what he made for me. He walked me home singing a Blind Lemon Jefferson song. I don't remember what it was, but I remember his voice.

It reminded me of Magic Al's voice that day he died. It sounds like the way you did when you sang to me when I was a child.

You sang, 'Never forget. Never forget.'

Your daughter,
Lorraine

22 July, 1964

Dear Daddy,
Mama always told me that you died when I was a little girl. She said that you died far away. When I asked her where, she just never said.

When we first moved to this house, the train a couple of blocks away would wake me up at night. Then I would imagine it was bringing you back to us. You would come in the door looking just like you did that day I saw you when I was ten. I haven't told Mama about that day. I promised I wouldn't.

Once when Mama and I went to the fairground, a gypsy woman told her that I was going on a long journey. She said that the journey would last a long time. She said that I would take Mama, too. She said that I was filled with the spirits of my ancestors. She said that the spirits with me were wandering spirits.

Mama told her that she was a devil. She told me never to talk to that lady again. But you know how it is when you know in your heart something is true.

Let me tell you something.

Two months ago, I started standing by the tavern on the next street. I just started standing there watching the cars go by. I don't know why. But I just stood there, thinking about where they were going. Oh Daddy, I dream about things moving. Moving, moving, moving all the time. Moving far away, out into the world, way out into the world. And me inside those moving things watching the world, and sometimes being in the world, too.

These are my days: Up at six. Wash up. Iron my uniform blouse. Comb my hair. I'm good at combing it without a mirror because lately I can't see anything in it anyway. Then I have some toast with Mama. We sit at the big table and listen to the farm reports on the radio even though we don't live on a farm. But I like to listen to them because I can see the open spaces when they talk. Then we both pray. Mama is into the Book Of Revelations now, and she reads something to me from it every day. I can still hear her voice when I'm sitting in that cold church during Mass before school.

I can hear her even when the priest is speaking.

School, well, I go from class to class. Sometimes I meet my friends and we skip a class. We go out and sit in the candy store and drink pop and talk about boys.

We're all there. The white girls on one side of the room, us on the other. I know we want to know about each other. But we never really speak. We just stare. Just stare.

I have to write to you because I have no one else to talk to. There is so much I want to say.

Tonight I saw a man die. He was a blues singer called Magic Al. He just got up to sing, then he fell over dead. I should have known something was going to happen today because today Mama got up singing the blues. And we did not pray. That's the first time she's done that since she became a preacher.

Today I stood on my corner as usual. But today I also left that corner. I got into a car with a stranger. He was a white man from France. He said his name was Claude. That was all I could understand.

Claude took me to a blues-club. That's how I saw Magic Al die.

When Magic Al dropped dead, he hit the floor and knocked his gold tooth out. It rolled right to my feet. I picked it up, and put it in my pocket. I think I should confess to the priest that I stole something. I mean, I think I did. But I couldn't give Magic Al his tooth back. He was dead.

Then a man jumped up speaking in tongues. Claude started speaking French. I left. Outside it seemed like everything was very bright. It still seems that way. Big, and bright and shiny. And my room seems very small now. Everything I know seems very small.

This is what I wish: I wish that I could take this gold tooth, go to the top of the tallest building in Chicago, hold that tooth up and tell everyone that I saw Magic Al die. I do. When he was lying there, I wanted to kiss him. I wanted to tell him that it was all over, and that everything was alright.

I have another secret. Why is life so full of secrets?

Right now I wish that I was with you. Because I know that you are living your life. I wish that Mama could be with you, too. We could all start over the way parents and kids should. Then I would not do whatever I did to make you go away, and take my face with you.

I remember you. You used to come home, and sit down, and Mama would have your food ready. You and Mama seemed so calm. Even when I was a little girl, I always liked to see you and Mama together because you looked so calm and happy. Like you always wanted to be a mother and father.

I want Mama to be proud of me. I want to do what she wants me to do. I'm sorry that I did what I did. I'm sorry that I went off with that white man. From now on, I'll always do what Mama wants.

I pray every night. I pray that I don't ever do anything wrong. I pray that I go to heaven. I pray that I see you again, and that you see me. When I get to heaven, I want to see you there and Mama, too. Then we can all be together. We'll never separate.

The nuns say that it is not possible to know everything. Once when I was a little girl I said that I understood the Holy Trinity, but the Sister said that I didn't because it was a mystery. Now I don't understand it anymore.

Kiss me, kiss me, kiss me, dear Daddy, wherever you are. I'm scared right now. What if I do see you and you don't even know me? What if we pass in the street and we don't even know it? That would be the worst thing in the world.

Sometimes I look up at the sky and think to myself that this is the same sky that Jesus saw, and that you saw. That is a very wonderful thing. But I don't have anybody to tell it to. So I'm writing to you.

I have to go now. I have a geography lesson to study. They say that there are parts of the world that people still have not explored. That's like our insides, too. My insides are open now, and I can't close them up anymore. No more. It's too late for me.

Everyone who sees me will think I'm the same. But I'm not. I'm like an alien. I'm like a piece of dust with no real home. I can see things pass right through me like I'm made of air.

There is so much I want to know about you and Mama. What it was like before I was born. I wish there was a movie house you could go to where they showed you stuff you couldn't see. Like the way George Burns used to go up to his room and watch this television set where he could spy on Gracie and Harry Vonzell.

In my movie house I could look at you. I could know everything.

Daddy, I will find you. My magic movie house will tell me where you are.

Your daughter,
Lorraine

oswald and elvira:
the movie

If there were such a thing as a kind of magic cinema, a place where it would be possible to see events that happened before our time, events that for better or worse irrevocably shaped us, then this would be the film Lorraine Williams would see in her magic cinema:

Fade up. Blues sound track. The sound of the Mississippi Delta of the twenties and early thirties. The sound of a black boy growing up.

The sound of her father Oswald Williams.

Sound was important to Oswald. All kinds of sound. For instance he liked to listen to the river. His uncle told him that if he listened well and listened hard, he could hear the voices of the river goddesses Yemanja, and Oshun.

The river was also a means of transport. He loved the idea of movement, too, the sounds of transport. He would love them his entire life.

These sounds included the long, low whistle of the north-bound trains of his childhood, the sound of the troop-transport of his youth crossing the English Channel heading for Normandy. Even as he gagged because of the roughness of the crossing mixed with the taste of the white amphetamine shoved down his throat, he still loved the sound.

He knew the names of all the trains that passed through: the 'Santa Fe,' 'Rock Island,' 'Texas and Pacific,' the 'Wabash,' 'Baltimore and Ohio,' the 'Chesapeake and Ohio,' 'Atlantic Coast,' 'Southern,' 'Chicago Great Western,' and the 'Chicago Northwestern,' the 'Seabord Line,' the 'Missouri-Pacific,' 'Louisville-Nashville,' 'St Louis-San Francisco,' 'Missouri-Kansas-Texas,' and the mighty 'Illinois Central' which would take him directly to Chicago, the land of the blues, the land of promise.

For the blues was the underpinning of it all. The blues was everything that ever was and everything that would be. The blues was travelling music, wandering music. No one had to tell him that.

Oswald's mother had a mirror which a peddler had told her belonged to Lillie Langtry, the Jersey Lily, who used to be the mistress of the King of England.

Oswald gazed into that mirror whenever he had the free time. He imagined that he could see that place called Jersey, an island far away from the drudgery and boredom of his own life. Some day he would play the blues and see it all.

Oswald's eyes troubled him from an early age. He knew eventually that he would go blind like his uncle Lucius. It was said that the men on his father's side had the gift of second sight. The blindness enabled them to 'see' more. But Oswald also knew from an early age that he would never follow in the illustrious footsteps of his father and his uncle, prophets renowned for their wisdom. He knew that his blindness was just that and nothing more. He thought himself far too ordinary. He would never have visions. That's why he intended to see everything he could before he could no longer see at all.

Before he died of giving too much and taking on other people's troubles, Oswald's father told him that he had gone down to the woods. Walking along, he saw a pair of eyes shining at him from a rock at the crossroads. He knew immediately who it was: Elegba, the god of the crossroads, sometimes known as the Devil.

Elegba had granted him a vision: the sight of his granddaughter walking through a leafy green park. She was grownup and carrying the pieces of a shattered mirror in her hand, her feet barefoot and bleeding, her eyes clouded over as if she were blind. And he, Oswald, was there, too, waiting for her. Waiting for his child. The park was on another continent. Far away.

That was the part Oswald liked. Another continent. He didn't want a child. A child tied you up too much.

The day after his mother died, he went into the Army. It was in the middle of the War. He was sent to a boot camp where the German prisoners-of-war protested at having to eat in the same mess hall as the black soldiers and the black soldiers protested at the preferential treatment the POWs were receiving. Several black soldiers were locked up. A small riot occurred. A few of them were killed. The Army told their relatives that they died in various mishaps.

To Oswald it was all insane. How could prisoners live better than soldiers who were serving their country? He taught himself the harmonica, the devil's harp, as a way of sorting it out for himself. Whenever he played the blues he could understand things.

He was stationed in England where he met airmen from the Caribbean. They fought almost nightly with the white GIs who taunted them for dating English girls. Oswald envied their freedom and their brashness. They were bluesmen, although they knew nothing about the blues.

For if he was indeed destined to have a child, that was what he wanted her to be. A blueswoman.

After the War, Oswald went to Chicago and took a job as a sleeping-car porter. That would keep him on the move. He liked his cap and jacket, too. It made him anonymous.

Once he saw a small black girl standing on a street corner near Dearborn Station in Chicago. She was wide-eyed and beautiful. She had the blues all around her. She contained in her small black body all the blues queens he used to see in their tent shows, resplendent in diamonds and slicked back hair. When he was a boy.

Resplendent and glorious and defiant and wild. Women no one could tie down. Women who stayed on the move. Blues queens.

And he knew just as well as he had known anything in his life that for a brief moment he had been given the second sight his father and his father before him had. He had been given the vision that he believed he would never see. His own child. This was his own daughter, the child who would be born to him.

As he watched her, it seemed as if all the sound around them disappeared, and there was only a silence, a silence so light, so delicate. A kind of blues silence, filled with poignance.

It reminded him of the essential innocence, the primal virginity of black women. That even the most worldly of them was imbued with an untouched spirit. Black women were always poised on the brink of something he could never know. Something unrealizable in this world. It's what made them age so slowly. Made them virgin.

Could he hear her name, too? Was it . . . Lorraine? Lorraine. When he said that name the world suddenly began to move again. And the child was gone.

The vision brought tears to his eyes. This child was inevitably tied to him. She was the continuation of his own life, his immortality.

She would carry him, and all that he himself could not carry.

Now all that was left was the appearance of her mother.

Blackout
Fade up. Brilliant color. Not the colors of nature.

Elvira Taylor hated nature. You could only find nature in the country. Elvira Taylor did not want to be associated with the country. The country meant loud-talking, tobacco chewing, nappy-headed women who had too many babies, and too few men. No. Lorraine's mother's color would be the garish tones of Technicolor. Nothing less would do.

The sound would be different from her father's, too. Movie sound tracks: Erich Korngold. Max Steiner, Alfred Newman, Bernard Hermann, Miklos Rosza. Her only concession toward anything approaching her own reality would be the music of Sonny Boy Williamson.

In spite of herself, she had a thing for the master harp player from Tennessee.

In her segment of the film Elvira would appear Lena Horne-like, leaning alone against a white column, so that, like Lena, her segment of the film could be cut out when it was distributed in the South.

All around her would be her favorite paintings, all by Degas: *L'Absinthe*, the portrait of the lonely drunk, gazing into the distance; *Ellen Andrée*, the same model, her eyes filled with longing, and most important to her of all, *Lala Au*

Cirque Fernando, *Paris*, the black acrobat so strong that she could hang by her teeth.

Elvira wanted to do all the things she was told she couldn't do: become a great painter, and meet the future Queen of England. She and Elizabeth had been born in the same year on the same day. Elvira thought they even looked alike.

The walls of her bedroom were covered with pictures of the Princess. Elvira even took a job during the War servicing jeeps because the Princess worked on jeeps. She had her hair tortuously straightened and curled to match the Princess's.

On Sundays, after she had managed to escape the boring routine of all day service, she dressed up in the flowery dresses she saw the Princess wear in Life Magazine and went to visit Sam Medoff's antique shop.

She would gingerly walk through the dusty tables piled high with all manner of European debris. She wore a hat and white gloves, which she prided herself on not soiling. She knew that old Medoff enjoyed her company because he was lonely on Sundays with everyone in church. He told her stories about his childhood in Vienna while she drank sweet tea from ancient china cups.

She loved the stories. She would imagine herself sitting in some tiny café on the Danube, listening to the urbane gossip of the elegant Jews whom Medoff deeply missed.

Yet she would not allow him to see the yearning in her eyes whenever he spoke about the places he had been. He was a white man after all (even though her mother had once said something about the Jews not exactly being white). She did not allow him to see, too, how he flattered her whenever he told her she was pretty. He might want something. After all, white or black, a man was a man.

Medoff flattered her not because he was handsome. He wasn't. It was because he had seen so much, knew so much, and been to so many places.

One Easter, just after the War, when she had taken a job in the local dime-store to appease her father, she left service early and as usual went to Medoff's. It was a warm day and he was seated out front in an old armchair. The chair was made of plush velvet and looked as if it had graced some drawing room long ago. He greeted her as he always did, and then told her that he had a present for her.

He took her to the back of the store. She had never been to the back before. For a moment she was gripped with terror. She remembered the stories she used to hear about how the Jews killed children and ate them at their services. She thought she smelled something cooking that she didn't recognize. She almost turned back. But she could not resist following him. She had to see what he had.

In the gloom, he produced a very large book. It was dusty and the dust got on her new dress. He led her back out into the light. He opened the book and showed her her first painting.

'Mademoiselle Lala,' he said, 'by Degas. You ever heard of him?'

She was tired of white people always thinking that colored people were stupid. So she lied and said of course she had. He gave the book to her. He touched her hands as he did so. His hands were warm, the warmest hands she had ever felt. They sent something through her body. She left very quickly before she could identify what the feeling was.

She studied the book from cover to cover, especially the painting of the black circus acrobat. She could see herself seated in the grandstand, looking up at the woman with the cannon dangling from her feet, twirling and twirling above the heads of the spectators.

What, she thought, would it be like to hang above the world? At night she dreamt she was Lala. Not only the seen, but because of her elevation, the seer. The power of the seer. The power of Degas. The power of a painter.

Yet she wondered what if the tables had been turned and Lala had painted Degas instead. What would she have made of the strange white man who watched her intently night after night? If only Elvira could express that point of view on canvas, be allowed to express it. Then she would have real power.

She stopped going to the movies and bought paints instead. She locked herself in her room, and made a small corner for herself near the window. She took the picture of Lala and studied it as closely as she could. She made what she called 'studies', her interpretations, and only permitted her aunt and her best friend Millie to see them.

Her father insisted that she spend more time with the Bible. She was destroying his reputation by her failure to attend service. She decided that the only escape was marriage. She had to find a man to take her away. Take her to Paris and the Cirque Fernando where a great painter fell in love with a black acrobat.

She was convinced that some day she would meet the future Queen of England, who would surely be her patron, and that she would live with a man who would allow her to do as she liked. This surely was her destiny.

And since we are watching Lorraine's movie, it is important that her parents 'meet cute' in true Hollywood movie fashion.

Elvira had gone one rainy day to Dearborn Street Station to meet a cousin coming in from California. She had seen him only once before when they were both twelve years old. He was due home on leave and was just stopping over while changing trains. She saw a man alight from the train who she thought was her cousin. But it was Oswald.

He did not dissuade her.

He took her for coffee in the station, although he knew that this was a futile thing to do. The waitress refused to serve them. Welcome back to the land of the free and the home of the brave, he thought to himself.

He told the waitress off in his version of a perfect English accent, the one he had acquired during the War. Everyone turned around. Elvira saw the expression on the waitress's face. She knew what the woman was thinking, that maybe this wasn't just some ordinary nigger, maybe he was an African prince. This is what she was thinking, too. This meant that he had seen something other than Chicago, or Mississippi. This meant he could take her places.

The waitress cursed them. Soon the police would arrive. But Elvira didn't care. Nat 'King' Cole was singing 'Sweet Lorraine' on the jukebox. By then Elvira knew that Oswald was not her cousin. By then she knew that they were going to marry.

She asked him to marry her the next day under the rococo Marshall Fields Department Store clock. He took a big gulp and said yes.

Elvira spent the entire night before their trip to City Hall on her knees praying that Oswald would take her away to Paris where she could paint, where they could make meals on a hot plate overlooking the Luxembourg Gardens. Where they could be just like Bogie and Bergman in *Casablanca*.

She married against her parents' wishes. She liked that. Her father did not attend the ceremony. Instead he went down to Maxwell Street and preached against the bluesmen and blueswomen who gathered there on Sunday. He preached against his new son-in-law, too, who lived there. She liked that, too.

Elvira loved the fact that Oswald lived on Maxwell Street. That he knew Big Bill Broonzy, the two Sonny Boy Williamsons, almost everyone who sang the blues in Chicago. He had promised to take her to all the blues clubs. She would learn every song. Then she could sing the blues in Paris by night, and paint in the day. Why not? Post-war Paris was wide open. She would be exotic, interesting, brilliant. Oswald would help. After all, he could talk like Ronald Colman if he wanted to.

Her mother warned her that a Mississippi man was not a good man to marry. She was from Alabama and she should know. Mississippi men had itchy feet. Elvira couldn't deny it. She was learning her blues. Hadn't Robert Johnson, Mississippi born and raised, sung about a 'hellhound on my trail?'

They spent their first night together in a small room in a friend's boarding house. She undressed as Oswald waited in the communal bathroom.

The whole thing was worse then she expected. He was clumsy, and she did not like it. She would never like it. But she would do it again if it got her to Paris.

To please her parents, they moved into Elvira's old room until they could afford a place of their own. Elvira was pleased because she managed to get pregnant right away. It wasn't in her plan, but at least he would leave her alone. They would take the baby with them. They would manage somehow.

But most miraculous of all, she was expecting at the same time the Princess Elizabeth was. This was some kind of omen.

In the early morning of 1 June 1948, Elvira waited outside

the Plantation Club. Sonny Boy Williamson was appearing there. She loved Sonny Boy Williamson. Elvira sat outside the club with Millie in Millie's blue coupé, the result of her blossoming recording career. She was becoming so famous that even Howlin' Wolf, that great assessor of potential rivals, was said to be interested in her.

Millie was not happy. A budding blues queen did not wait in dark alleys for anyone. 'You don't catch Princess Elizabeth doin' nothin' like this,' she snarled, sucking on her Camel. Even that made no impression on Elvira. She must meet Sonny Boy. Sonny Boy knew something about her, something that she herself could not understand. Perhaps he could tell her a way to escape the life she was rapidly falling into.

She had rehearsed everything in her mind. She would introduce herself to the bluesman, ask for his autograph, then ask him about the origin of some of her favorites: 'Insurance Man Blues,' 'My Black Name,' and most especially the Devil song. The ice-pick imagery of it had been haunting her for several nights. She would mention that to him.

The bluesman emerged from the club alone, carrying his two harmonicas. Elvira followed him into the alley, keeping a discreet distance. She was wearing Millie's fox chubbie to disguise her stomach. She held her head high, exactly the way Princess Elizabeth did in the newsreels.

Suddenly, the air seemed to change. She could smell her own perfume, feel the sweat bead on her forehead drop by drop. A low, dull sound whirled in her brain. Something was about to happen.

Sonny Boy stopped as two men darted from the shadows. Suddenly he fell to the ground. He had been stabbed several times – with an ice-pick.

She heard his death moan: 'Lord, have mercy Lord have mercy.'

That incantation was a message to her. She had strayed too far. She had gone to the Devil, and away from God. How could she have been so foolish? But God, in His mercy, had taken another life in order to give her eternal life. The Lord giveth and the Lord taketh away, even someone as well-loved as Sonny Boy.

Now she knew. Her journey was not to some foreign country, living the life of a sinful bohemian. It was right here, in Chicago, among her own people, leading them away from sin.

She vowed that night in the dark, blood-stained alley to dedicate her life to God, and to dedicate the life of the child she was carrying, too.

Whether that child liked it or not.

The day after Sonny Boy's funeral, Elvira became a deacon. She destroyed all of her blues records. She poured her paints down the toilet. She got rid of everything; except one small box which she kept hidden.

Elvira gave birth to Lorraine in an Anglican missionary hospital. On the day she was due, for the last time, Elvira dressed up. She looked like Joan Crawford in the last reel of *Mildred Pierce*.

Elvira marched behind the waddling, little nun who admitted her, the sound of the Carmen Miranda platforms she bought especially for the occasion like drumbeats on the highly polished floor. African imagery decorated every nook and cranny of the hospital. The nun pointed them out as they passed.

Elvira was polite, but insulted. She could not understand how anyone could possibly believe that she could be interested in the jungle. She was much more interested in the signed photo of the Royal Family that hung in the entrance to the hospital.

Lorraine's birth was slow and difficult. Labor left Elvira drained and humiliated. She did not like the loss of control over her body. When she was given the small, wiggly, brown bundle, she flinched as Lorraine's tiny mouth locked on her nipple. Instead of warmth, Elvira was overwhelmed with revulsion.

Nat 'King' Cole sang 'Sweet Lorraine' on the radio when the child was first brought to her. It was the same song that had been playing when she knew Oswald was going to be her husband. A sign. Elvira named her daughter Lorraine. But she looked too much like Oswald. She could barely stand to look at her.

She was annoyed that she had missed the free layette service awarded to the mother who gave birth on the day the Princess Elizabeth did. Elvira had tried to delay Lorraine, but she couldn't. Her daughter did exactly as she pleased.

Oswald was away off and on for the next five years. Lorraine could not really remember what he looked like, just some fleeting presence who came and went mysteriously in the night, and for whom an extra plate was set with elaborate ceremony.

After he had gone, her mother seemed to pray more than usual. Lorraine often wondered what caused her to do that.

One day while playing, she saw a man watching her from a car parked across the street. Eventually he came up to her. He was carrying a beautiful mirror. She knew who he was. He was her father. She could feel it.

He gazed for a moment up at the window of her mother's apartment. Lorraine saw the curtain move.

He handed her the mirror, but because she was a little girl and clumsy, she dropped it. It shattered in a million pieces. Her father got into his car, drove away, and out of her life.

Fade out. The movie ends in Lorraine's magic cinema. The film that would tell her everything she yearned to know, the film that would somehow make sense of her life.

And just as she is enjoying her newly found enlightenment, the lights would come on abruptly. Once again, Lorraine would find herself an outsider in the world. A prisoner of real life.

Real life. Real life was the tidy bungalow her mother's burgeoning congregation had scraped together to house their founder and pastor. It had once belonged to a white family who had made a hasty exit when they realized that they could not stop the tide of change.

It was painted a dull brown, and had window boxes. The backyard was neatly arranged in a mindless 'Father knows best' fashion with carefully mown grass and a barbecue grill. There was a white alabaster marble Greek statue in the midst of it all. Lorraine liked the statue, but her mother had it pulled down because it looked too 'pagan.'

The only time Lorraine caught sight of her neighbors on either side was when a few of the Brothers from the Tabernacle came over to dismantle the statue and the neighbors stood around and watched.

Their sullen white faces were closed and tight, as if in pulling down the statue, a part of them was being violated.

Lorraine nicknamed the family on her right the Frankenstein Family because they all, including the wife, seemed to have square heads and set jaws, and those on her left The Body Snatchers because she was sure, with their suburban perfection, that they were simply not real.

Lorraine was used to the hustle and bustle of what was increasingly being called 'the ghetto' although she had no idea what the word ghetto meant. It had just been the place she lived in.

Her new community was too quiet, too secretive. Sometimes at night, particularly in the summer, the quiet would explode as white boys in souped up cars rode past and threw rocks at their windows.

Those were the times her mother would pull her down on her knees and make her pray for their souls. This never made sense to Lorraine. Were *they* praying for *her* soul? Somehow she doubted it. She doubted that they prayed at all. They just spent the hot summer days planning their next assault. If she'd been a big man like Muhammed Ali, she would have confronted them and beat them within an inch of their lives.

Instead, she decided she would spend her life crusading against those blond barbarians who thought themselves the centre of everything.

Then one day something happened which taught her about the existence of the unknown.

The Body Snatchers were having a garage built. Lorraine sat on the back porch reading a school book when she noticed one of the workers. He was blond, not very tall, with clear blue eyes. The hair on his muscular arms was golden, and he never spoke, not even when his co-workers spoke to him. She overheard one of them saying that he was retarded, that he was the foreman's nephew, that he thought he was too good, etc.

She became obsessed with the way his skin gradually darkened every day in the summer sun. The way the golden hairs on his arms grew lighter every day.

She would sit outside all day in the shade of the porch, sometimes forgetting to eat, pretending to read her Latin grammar, or study algebra, watching him. Her enemy.

He was not beautiful. He was not as beautiful as Winston. Winston was tall and brown with a slender waist and eyes like a fawn. This man looked cruel, old before his time, wasted.

Yet she dreamt not of Winston, but of him. She imagined that he lived further south, in the working-class districts where the sons and daughters of Polish immigrants lived. She imagined his house, too, dark, small, and cluttered. Completely devoid of light, of books, of music. He ate lunch meat sandwiches with mayonnaise on white bread. He spoke Polish at home and watched the Cubs play baseball in summer and the Black Hawks play ice hockey in the winter. He would especially like ice hockey because ice hockey was a fight where sometimes a game took place.

He had probably been brought up to hate her. Her people competed with his people for jobs, for housing, for respect. He might even be among the boys who rode the streets at night terrorizing the few black families who had dared move in.

Yet, in spite of all she knew, all history taught her must be true, yet – she held imaginary conversations. With him. She taught him the Gallic Wars, and Gregorian chant.

He taught her how to deal with the basic things: food, clothing, shelter, light, air. Life.

Whenever her mother caught her sitting on the porch, she would be ordered back inside. Elvira would always find something for her to do until the workmen packed up and went home. Then when he was gone, Lorraine would stare for a long time at the space he stood in as he dug the ground.

Now, at almost fifteen, she felt herself fighting against something that was beginning to close in around her. She had started to gain weight at thirteen, and her mother promptly put her inside a girdle. She said that nice girls didn't 'jiggle.' By now Lorraine's breasts and behind were encased in white whalebone, her body deodorized, her hair straightened.

She had to help out at the Tabernacle more, assisting at the tank during baptisms, arranging the Bible studies, etc. Sometimes she visited people with her mother, sitting quietly in the background as Elvira exorcised a devil or tried to save a marriage.

Something was closing around her. She could see it in the few black girls who attended her school. It was the Mantle of Respectability.

She, along with the others, was the product of a dream. They were expected to carry a race on their back, expected to honor their history, to be better than any black woman who had gone before. There was no questioning this. Only death or madness could liberate her from her destiny.

They were watching her now, watching her for signs of waywardness, incorrectness. Lorraine laughed at the supposition that black people were lewd, loose and lazy. Black people were as tightly wound as anyone could be. Sex was a topic no one discussed except to point out its consequences. And black people worked like dogs. The Emancipation Proclamation, someone said, didn't free black people. It fired them.

She could be a part of the Great Plan, look thirty at twenty (carrying an entire race on your back was a major factor in premature ageing), marry respectably, then eventually take over her mother's Tabernacle. And she would surely disappear, not only to the world, but to herself.

She would be like her own mother, who kept an easel with a blank canvas in the corner of her bedroom, and was always pouring the whiskey down the sink undrunk that she brought home in moments of despair.

Her mother who was odorless, colorless, and tasteless, unless you counted the odor of sanctity, the color of church white, and the taste of nothing.

Now was the time to go if she were ever to escape this. But go where? She was barely fifteen. JFK had been assassinated. What kind of world would she go into? She did not understand the thing in her that urged her to move on. It grew stronger and stronger everyday. It caused her to stand on the corner at the mouth of the expressway every day after school, her uniform hidden beneath her coat in the winter, or disguised beneath a dress in the summer.

She stood there because there people were moving. They were going somewhere. Somewhere else.

For the blond workman taught her one thing: that she, Lorraine Williams, wanted to know The Other. She didn't need a show-all movie in some magic cinema to tell her that.

For the familiar was just that: the familiar. Even at fifteen, Lorraine could not see how anyone could know themselves unless they knew The Other. And she wanted to know herself.

She knew she was on a dangerous path. An incorrect, hell-bent path. But she stood on the corner anyway. She had no other choice.

Someday someone driving past would give her a lift into the unknown, into the world beyond.

To The Other.

Chicago
Summer of 1964

When Lorraine woke up on the morning that changed her
life, she knew instantly that she was not going to school.

It was a humid, sticky Midwest summer morning, the kind
of morning that was boiling hot by eight o'clock and you
could fry an egg on the sidewalk, as the old people used to
say.

She sat up as if on fire. There was something on fire in
her today. Something was going to happen today. She listened
for Elvira's gospel records and the crackle of eggs and bacon
in the kitchen. Everything seemed normal.

She felt her scalp. It was 'fry and lay to the side time'
again. Soon she'd have to go to the hairdressers and subject
herself to Mrs Pritchard and her lye. She didn't know which
she loathed the most: the white, thick mixture which made
her hair straight as a Chinese, or the boastful Mrs Pritchard
who called black people 'nigs' and kept an elegant hand pistol
in her drawer.

Today everything seemed more electric, more alive, as if
some fairies had done their work at night, giving everything
a kind of 'suchness.'

She took her bath, then joined Elvira at table. Her mother

was deep into the Gospel according to St John and barely noticed her. This was good. It enabled her to slip away unnoticed.

'Good mornin', darlin',' the Crystal Twins chirped as she passed by. Her mother, in one of her uncharitable moments, referred to the twins as charter members of the 'blue vein' society because they were so light-skinned, you could see the veins on their wrist.

This fascinated Lorraine. There had been a girl in her kindergarten who had long, silky braids and light, very delicate wrists. Lorraine stared at the blue veins criss-crossing their way beneath the skin of an obviously very special person. She didn't have that kind of skin.

'Come over here, Lorraine, honey, just for a minute. We want to show you something.'

If one Crystal Twin spoke, the other one finished the sentence. It was creepy, but Lorraine was taught always to be polite and obedient to adults, so she came over as she was told.

'Goin' to school, baby?' one of them asked.

'All girls' school is unnatural,' the other one said. 'A girl your age needs boys . . .'

'. . . to let you know what it means to be a girl.'

They then pulled her close to them. She could smell the talcum between their breasts.

'Your daddy knew that,' one of them whispered.

A chill went through Lorraine's body. Her daddy? Did they say her daddy?

'Yes he did,' they chorused.

'Child, you should know everything.'

'We knew your daddy, Oswald Williams, a long time ago . . . He used to . . .'

'. . . be the sleeping-car porter whenever Truman's daughter . . .'

'. . . got on the train. Whenever she did. She really . . .'

'. . . naw, it wasn't her. It was somebody else. Somebody who worked for Margaret Truman. You know. She came . . .'

'. . . to the club a lot. Not Margaret Truman. The woman who worked for her. Loud heifer. Child, that white lady . . .'

'. . . always wore dead birds in big hats, Lord, she . . .'

'. . . farted a lot, I swear, but lady-like . . .'

'. . . poot-poot. Uh-huh.'

'Oswald Williams. Your daddy. We saw him. Yeah. Pretty . . .'

'. . . colored man. So pretty he make you want to cry . . .'

'. . . make you want to lick him all over . . . oh, 'scuse us, baby, . . . we were sure surprised when we found out that he got married and that . . .'

'. . . he married a preacher-woman . . .'

'. . . I mean your mama, 'scuse us, baby.'

Lorraine had never known before that moment that practically right across the street lived two people who had known her father.

'You look just like him, you just a little tall and heavy. Your daddy's a delicate man. Who you take after?'

It was all too much. Whether it was the blazing heat or the shock of the news, before she could stop herself, Lorraine had run down the street as far as she could. Right to the 'Rib Shack.'

'The Rib Shack' looked like a frontier outpost. It had a fake log cabin design. The entrance was a real log door that suddenly appeared one day by truck from Iowa. It was generally acknowledged that this was the result of proceeds from 'policy,' the game that ran among those who considered themselves still a part of the old neighborhoods they had left behind.

The smell of barbecue filled the air day and night. Everything and everyone who was considered not respectable came there. Lorraine was forbidden ever to set foot there on pain of a severe beating.

Today was the day she made up her mind to go inside.

Paris was there today. From outside, Lorraine could see her at her usual post: right underneath the poster of Dorothy Dandridge, considered the most beautiful black woman in the world. Dandridge advertised 'Kayro Syrup,' the pancake syrup all the famous black people used every morning on their pancakes.

Lorraine liked Dorothy Dandridge, but she thought Paris was the most beautiful woman in the world. She was the color of mahogany, and always wore the brightest colors, the purest, strongest colors. Paris would occasionally, with the most elegant gesture, examine her face in the small compact mirror she always carried. It was as if she was composing her face, reinventing it every time.

'There's always a bad black woman somewhere, on every street,' Elvira said whenever Paris passed by. 'She's the Devil's woman come to test you on how close you are to God.'

Maybe she was going to be a bad woman, too. Today in the heat and the smell of the barbecue, she believed it could happen.

When Lorraine peered through the smoky windows of the barbecue house that day, Paris motioned her inside. Lorraine shook her head. Someone might see her. Paris got up and came outside. Without a word, she led Lorraine around the back, and out into the bushes, out beneath the trees known as 'ghetto palms.' The dirt and broken glass barely touched Paris's shoes. Today Paris seemed to walk on air.

Paris pulled out a flask and put it to Lorraine's lips. It was her first drink. She liked the way it felt as it slipped down her throat. She liked the way it made her head feel. Her body which felt to her lumpy and out of control, growing too quickly in all the wrong places, was suddenly as small and as delicate as Paris's own.

'Don't never overdo alcohol, understand?'

'Yes, ma'am. What it is?' Lorraine asked as she reached for more.

'Champagne,' Paris whispered.

Lorraine put her mouth to the flask, right on the place where Paris's lipstick imprint was, and took a deep, long drink. Champagne. She drank again. This was the true holy water, a thousand times more redemptive than what was in church.

And as the champagne danced down her throat, as if a thousand moon beams had found refuge there. The cloudless Chicago sky seemed to envelop everything. This sky, she thought to herself, that everyone who has ever lived has seen. Even the trees sparkled. It was like the elevation of the golden monstrance at high Mass. She wanted to genuflect. Instead she whispered '*Saecula saeculorum.*' 'World without end.'

And then she saw it. The inherent joke in everything. Behind it all, Someone was laughing. Not in a derisive way. But in the way a child laughs, delighted with all of creation. Lorraine giggled too. She took another drink. And another. Then she danced back inside the infamous 'Rib Shack' with the most infamous woman in town.

Paris led her back to the table beneath the Dorothy Dandridge poster. Lorraine sat down and closed her eyes. Closed them so that she could listen to the music in the voices of the people around. The sweet music that up until this moment she had taken for granted all her life. And when she opened her eyes, everything seemed to swim in the sweetness of the champagne, swim in the sweetness of the people and the way they did even the smallest thing with infinite grace and beauty.

It was turning out to be a wonderful day.

For that moment, it did not matter that she could not see herself. These people were herself. They were her father, too, and her mother. These people, who, in their way, had always loved her, had always been her eyes, her ears, her very self.

Just as she was about to rise and merge herself in some awkward gesture with the people, annihilate herself in their beauty, she saw a man standing in the doorway quite unlike the other men in the 'Rib Shack.' He was tall, his hair a dirty light brown colour, his eyes hidden behind small glasses. He had a slight paunch which was edging its way over his belt, his shoes were shiny, new, and foreign. He had a map in one hand and a damp phrase book in the other.

He asked for directions, but because he was white and a stranger, no one answered him. Something in Lorraine pulled her up from her seat. For the first time she felt Paris's restraining hand. That hand contained every moment of time that they, and those before them, had been on this continent. The weight of Paris's touch made her hesitate for a moment.

But the man had seen her take a step toward him, so he came over, his large eyes moist from the heat. 'I am lost,' he said very carefully. 'My name is Claude. What is yours?'

'Lorraine,' she replied, as if she had known him all her life. She was not sure he was even speaking English to her, but whatever he was speaking she understood. It was the clearest speech she had ever heard.

She knew who he was. This was the man come to take her into the Unknown.

'I seem to be lost,' he was saying, 'I'm looking for this address.' Paris snatched the piece of paper from his hand before Lorraine could see it. The atmosphere abruptly changed. The 'Rib Shack' was like a nuclear bomb thirty seconds to midnight. A few of the men had moved closer together in threatening clusters. Lorraine knew what could happen, but the champagne felt too good, and besides, she was much too fascinated by the way the men looked: Benin, Dahomey, all the ancient kingdoms were etched in their faces, each a once great nation in Africa, heirs of a people who had left their mark on everything they had touched. Left their mark on their sons, too, now gathering like warriors to eliminate an outsider.

'I know where you want to go,' Lorraine said suddenly. 'You got a car?'

'Yes,' the man named Claude said, his eyes like demented butterflies darting around the room.

'Let's go,' Lorraine boomed, to bolster their courage.

The very 'Rib Shack' itself seemed to quake from its foundations. This time Paris grabbed her so hard that Lorraine cried out. The sound of her own voice rang through her body like an alarm, steeling her, reminding her of what else old Cat-eye had said: 'You'll find your daddy, Lorraine, you'll find him on the road. Through a stranger.'

She left with Claude, out into the bright day, a small crowd following them out. Bobby Darin sang 'Somewhere Beyond the Sea' on someone's transistor radio. Yes, Lorraine thought, somewhere beyond the sea . . .

She sank into the plush seats of Claude's rented Thunderbird. She sniffed the aroma of new leather upholstery. She felt the cold steel and chromium, the purr of a car that felt as big as her bedroom. Claude was not used to all the power he had at his disposal. She laughed out loud as he touched the steering wheel, and the car shot off like a bat out of hell.

They sped off down the highway toward the lakefront, the other side of town. Past the gas stations with their huge American flags flying out front, past the funeral home with the drive-in window and the stark white hearses trimmed in gold, past the little store-front churches with the hand-painted signs, past her mother's brand new house of worship: the Tabernacle of Radiant Energy built as a mini Taj Mahal; past all of it, and deep into the canyon of downtown Chicago, and the shade of the skyscrapers, onto the snaky drive that ran along the lakefront.

The man told her his name again. Claude. He had come to Chicago to hear the blues. The blues was the only music in the world. Everything came from the blues. He told her about arriving at the airport, the sounds and different sights he had seen. How big Americans were, how expansive their gestures. And he had found a bluesman in the men's toilet, a man named Otis. Otis took him to his home on a street with old houses whose steps jutted out front like the chests of grand old dowagers. He smelled hair frying in the air, good food, and bad whiskey. He was led down a dark corridor whose cool marble floors reminded him of a brothel, and then into Otis's small room, crammed with memorabilia of Bessie and Ma Rainey, of Robert Nighthawk, the two Sonny Boys, Muddy Waters.

Otis told him about a man from Mississippi by the name of Magic Al who was the true heir of Robert Johnson and who sang the blues with a hat like a small sombrero, dressed all in black, and with a toothpick in his mouth.

His life had been dull and useless, Claude said, except for the time, when as a small boy after the Liberation, he had been befriended by two black GIs. There was one in particular by the name of Oswald who wiped his spoon in the most elegant gesture when offered a coffee by a woman who lived in the street.

He and Oswald had stood together alongside the equestrian statue of Henri Quatre on the Pont Neuf and sang the blues.

Lorraine held her breath for a moment. This was the second time her father had been mentioned today and it was still early yet! But she didn't want to ask him questions. This was a magic day and this magic man from Paris might not be real.

He might be a trick of Elegba because she had been at a kind of crossroads and had therefore been sent a vision. So she listened and allowed herself to be suspended between the two worlds and to live there, just as her great-Auntie Muriel had been suspended in her circus act, her mother suspended in her life; and she suspended, too, poised between childhood and womanhood!

She felt the cool lake breeze on her face as Claude accelerated to the sound of B. B. King's guitar. It felt as if she had known this man all her life, that he understood everything. But how could he? That wasn't meant to be. He was white and he was foreign.

There was something happening here that no one had prepared her for. Something happening that had defied everything she had ever seen, had ever been taught.

Life, mysterious, unpredictable. Life was not what someone else told you, not even what the nuns, or your best friend, your mama, or even God told you. It had to be experienced. On your own terms, in your own way.

For instance, she thought as they swept past the ornate buildings that sparkled like diamonds on the posh North Shore, how could anyone take the word of the Bible? How can we be sure that a bunch of crazy people didn't write it? How could we know if it was true unless we lived it, day by day, moment by moment? And even then everyone's experience would be different because everyone was different. Why were people afraid of people who were different?

And what was her mother doing, standing in a pulpit Sunday after Sunday, exhorting God to smite this one and that one? What was she looking for and what were the people who came to her looking for? How could Elvira really know about God if she couldn't fill that empty canvas in her bedroom, or open that small black box she kept hidden?

How could she know God if she had never once helped her own child look for her father?

She said these things to Claude. He listened then he told her that when he was a young boy, he had seen Jean Moulin, the Resistance leader, in Lyons. Moulin was half sitting, half lying on a bench, his body a mass of wounds. He was trying to see himself in a shop window. But he could barely keep his head up.

Years later Claude had asked his own mother if that were possible, and she told him that it would have been impossible. Moulin had disappeared. No one had seen him. The Gestapo had captured him and that was that.

But he had seen the man with his own eyes, and yet his own mother attempted to hide a truth he had discovered himself. It was then, Claude told her, that he realized that his whole country, the world, hid from the truth about itself.

That life itself was a series of obfuscations. That no one, including him, could really look themselves in the face. For to face oneself was to see, in spite of all the associations, the attempts at connectedness, that human beings are essentially and unalterably alone.

That was why he had turned to the blues.

There were tiny beads of sweat forming on Claude's lip. They made him look vulnerable, like a child. Lorraine liked children, so she leaned over and kissed him. She felt his breath hot on her face, and thought she felt his hand, too, rest lightly on her knee, but she could not be sure. Paris's champagne was dancing around inside her, conjuring up an entire universe, blue and whole from the vast shores of the lake before them.

What could she share with him? She had nothing more to say, except that she longed to see what he had seen. To hear his voice every day of her life. To extend this moment so that it stretched into eternity.

They passed Buckingham Fountain, a graceful mass of stone with great jets of colored water shooting up into the sky.

The last time she had seen it was with her mother when they had come to catch a glimpse of the Queen of England. The Queen walked right past them, her face warm but impassive, her bright pink flowered cloche hat catching the light.

Elvira dropped her camera because the Queen extended her hand to her. When Lorraine stooped to pick the camera up, she thought she saw what looked like her father moving slowly through the crowd.

She aimed her camera toward the man, her back to the Queen. Just as she was about to snap his picture, the police pounced on him. Someone in the crowd said that he had been picking pockets. She saw the police take him away, and beat him up in the bushes far away from the Queen.

Elvira sent Lorraine to bed without her supper because she had missed taking a picture of her shaking hands with Elizabeth. From then on, Lorraine had to celebrate Prince Charles's birthday. That was punishment enough.

In the cold, damp light of mid-November, Elvira would play the British national anthem (which was really 'My Country 'Tis of Thee', Lorraine realized), and wave British flags next to a small picture of the heir to the throne. Elvira, in deeply serious tones, would then read out all his titles: 'Prince of Wales, Duke of Cornwall, Baron Renfrew,' etc.

Lorraine would stand at attention, gazing at the flickering candles, listening to her mother's voice. It was at times like these that she knew Elvira wasn't really happy.

Lorraine and Claude stopped for a while on the beach to cool off. There he told her other stories about the blues queens he met in Paris in the fifties who stayed in rooms in the Rue de Rivoli and were friends of Colette. Their speciality was an act in which they portrayed all the great blues queens: Victoria Spivey, Ida Cox, Trixie Smith, Clary Smith and Sippie Wallace, and a dozen more he could not remember. Their signature tune was Mary Dixon's 'You Can't Sleep In My Bed.'

And then he sang for her, his voice surprisingly like the voices of the people she knew, complete with that trademark Delta growl like rolling thunder on a hot summer's day.

He taught her the Rimbaud he had taught them: 'Les blancs débarquent. Le canon! Il faut se soumettre au baptême, s'habiller, travailler.'

Lorraine said the words over and over to herself. She

translated them with the help of her highschool French: 'The white men are landing. The cannon. We must submit, to baptism, put on clothes, work.'

Three young black boys were splashing water on one another oblivious to the whites who were staring at them. Not long ago, even in her brief lifetime, blacks could not come to this beach. She remembered the images of black students wading in the surf in Florida, water soaking their clothing as they marched on the beach against segregation. Some ancient beach in Africa was where it had all begun with guns, and chains, crucifixes and mirrors.

He said to her: 'My father had a statue of the black Virgin. He kept it hidden away. I saw it one day, the day he came back to us. My lost father. He brought her with him from the woods. He had been hiding there after the Liberation. He had to. That Virgin was as black as night. She is found, they say, by serendipity. You must wander in order to find her. Not search. She is not on a deliberate route. My father called her 'La Retour.' La Retour had no face. This was so she could reflect back the inner truth of those who gazed upon her. May you find La Retour someday, Lorraine, so that She can reflect her truth to you . . .'

On the way to the blues club, he told her other things: of Peetie Wheatstraw, 'The Devil's Son-In-Law' and his Kansas City blues playing; the difference between the two men who called themselves Sonny Boy Williamson: the one from Tennessee now dead, the other from Mississippi and still alive; how to tell various styles of the blues: the easy-going Piedmont blues, the barrel-house New Orleans blues, the good-time, raucous Kansas City blues, the dark, haunted Mississippi blues.

He stressed that he was merely a connoisseur. This was her music, and thus she was the blues itself. 'Perhaps,' he said, 'this is why so many young Negroes like yourself are not interested. It is too close, too essential. It has no hope, only reality. In spite of everything, you are American. America is the land of eternal hope. So, it is very clear. The blues is not hopeful enough for you.'

Another thing was very clear, too. Lorraine Williams would have to see the world, the whole of it because the world contained people like this Frenchman. As she listened, she knew what she must do to prepare herself for the world: gorge herself with the blues, especially, Claude had said, the music of Robert Nighthawk, one of the greatest blues singers who had ever lived, and who was now singing on Sundays down on Maxwell Street like someone newly up from the South without any reputation.

They arrived at the club just as the sky turned a warm navy blue. The place was like a run-down garage. It had small glossy photos of the various acts pasted to the glass by masking tape. Some of the photos were at strange angles, blown askew by the stiff Chicago wind.

Magic Al's photo had almost been blown away. Lorraine gazed at his picture for a long time. She had never seen anyone quite like him before. His dark, grizzled face did not seem of this world. His black hat covered one eye. He looked evil, also very beautiful. And very definitely The Unknown.

While Claude tried to talk their way into the club, Lorraine walked around the back. She was still full of Paris's champagne, still full of Claude and his stories, still full of the prospect of life on the road in the big wide world full of blues.

Something led her across the graveled parking-lot to a little cabin. She knocked on the door, and Magic Al opened it.

He was the tallest person she had ever seen. He had his hat off, and there was a rim around his crown, his hair in uncombed clumps. He was trying to rake it with a wide-tooth comb which was too small for his gigantic fist. His body was lean, and his feet were also very big. He invited her inside as if he had ordered her up from a local take-away.

'You look like a schoolgirl,' he growled as he lit a small cigar. Well, that's what she was, Lorraine thought as she sat on the sagging camp bed. It made a strange sound as it practically sank to the floor. She stifled a nervous giggle and stared at his bottle of Scotch. He poured her a small drink in a Dixie-cup, and she drank it so quickly that she almost gagged. But it was a good gag, she decided, the kind that you have after sucking a sour grape candy. She would no longer have a taste for that after this.

'What you want?' he asked. His voice was full of music. She only shook her head because she did not want her voice to disturb the music that was still in the air.

'You goin' somewhere, ain't you? It's all over your face.' He sat down next to her. She could tell that he had been drinking all day. That was surely what aggravated the sad look in his eye, the way he held his head at a certain melancholy angle. This man had a great overwhelming sadness so tangible it was a separate part of him. It sat in the corner of the room, swaying and moaning back and forth.

He put his hand on her breast. His hand was like ice. It made her shiver. Lorraine instinctively moved away. He offered her another drink.

'You goin' somewhere, ain't you?' he repeated. 'Go to New York City. Tell you what. When you go, there's a tree in

New York City is like the Tree Of The Knowledge Of Good
And Evil. Now, it don't always yield up its secrets, but you
hit it at the right time and you'll know what you want to
know.'

'Will it tell me what happened to my father?'

'You'll know everything,' he said as he started to undo her
blouse.

All the time that she lay on her back, all the while that
she felt him plough into her, even in the midst of the
pain, she could see New York, the tree. New York was all
the knowledge in the world. Whatever she had to endure
was worth that information.

Whether she assisted him, or whether he just did what he
wanted, either way it did not matter. And in the midst of it,
she felt her own power. The power she had to make the
great man breathe as if he were drowning, his face almost
otherworldly.

Power. It was the power of her own body causing his to
melt deeper and deeper inside her. Power. This knowledge
made it stop hurting. Made her smile when he suddenly yelled
in pleasure and came on her belly.

Power. She knew that Magic felt it, too. Power was the
silence in the room. Magic wiped himself without saying a
word. She understood. All of this was routine to him. Her
power wavered a little. That dark, demonic look had
descended on his face again. She had nothing to match that.

She walked out into the pitch-black night, mesmerized by
the sound of her feet on the gravel.

Claude was waiting outside with a look of terror on his
face. 'Where have you been!' he screamed. She kissed him
very hard on the mouth, like a woman kissed, before he could

repeat the question. He followed her inside. She liked kissing him. It made him quiet. She could kiss anyone she wanted now. Do whatever she wanted now.

A drunk at the bar was complaining. 'Pussy-whipped,' he growled. It was going to be a woman's world soon, he warned. Lorraine smiled. She certainly hoped so. Then mothers wouldn't make some distant god up in the sky their husbands.

She said this to him, too.

That's how brave she felt.

As Lorraine finished her third whiskey, she thought about calling her mother. She thought about telling Elvira how much she hated their sterile existence, how she longed to live in New York where people were free. She rehearsed the call over and over in her head until Magic Al and his band came on.

Al acknowledged her with the coolest of glances. The audience held its collective breath. 'Magic Al' was introduced. He picked up his guitar, looked Lorraine straight in the eye, then promptly fell over. Dead. His gold tooth popped out of his mouth and landed at Lorraine's feet. Lorraine understood. Her power had killed him. His gold tooth was her homage.

Claude was swallowed up in the small crowd that surged to the front. She never saw him again.

Lorraine couldn't help it, but she made the sign of the cross as she walked out into the deep prairie night, the deep blue night only relieved by splashes of neon from the clubs and various 'joints' which lined the street. The street now so full of the hub of humanity, nocturnal humanity mingled together in the cool darkness.

There could be no doubt about it now. She knew she was not in fellowship with her mother's congregation, nor with the nuns and their plans for her vocation, either. She was one with the blues people who crowded the pavement on this hot summer night, some of them with backpacks, following the musicians from job to job. Nomads of the blues. These were her people.

She walked home. Once or twice the police stopped her, but they left her alone. She was propositioned, but nothing would take her from this hard freedom. Nothing.

When she got home, Elvira was rocking in her rocking chair reading the Bible. She did not look up. She was trembling and singing something low in her throat. It sounded like the blues.

One candle was burning and it was almost burned down. The light made her mother's shadow look like the biggest thing in the world. Bigger than the world itself. Lorraine did not dare move near it. It might swallow her up. Swallow her and make her stay in Chicago. Become her mother. Become like all of them.

'Mama, I saw a blues man die!' she blurted out as if showing off her exam results.

Elvira was quiet for a long time. There was no sound except the creak of the old chair, the wind blowing in the trees. When she did speak, her voice was dry and choked and small.

'Promise me this Lorraine. That you won't leave home before your thirtieth birthday. Just like Jesus did when he went into the desert to ask God's blessing for his ministry. Promise me. Promise you won't go until then.'

Elvira's eyes were desperate. Lorraine had never seen her mother like that before. She put her arms around her. They hugged one another in the old rocking chair.

How could she tell her mother that she had already gone? That she had left on an eastbound train and would never return? That no matter how long she stayed, she was not here. She was gone. Gone. Gone to those places her father must have seen, or Claude must have seen, or Magic Al. Her mother had seen nothing. But she, Lorraine, was gone. Gone.

She kissed her mother's face. It was as soft as a child's. Thirty. That felt like a hundred years away. And although it took everything in her to agree, she said yes. As she said it, she could feel the thing that she had tried to run away from close in on her. Envelop her as it was enveloping all her friends. Envelop her and never gorge her out. The Mantle of Respectability. But she could hold it at bay. She would do everything in her power to hold it at bay, not let it smother her, so that she could survive and leave for New York City.

the inaudible and noiseless foot of time

'Don't open your eyes yet,' Winston whispered as he crawled over Lorraine to open the window to let in the fresh air of the Michigan woods. But she peeped anyway. She peeped because she loved Winston's dark body, its quicksilver grace, its smell and strength. But most of all its vulnerability which he never wanted to acknowledge because he thought it was a thing a black man did not admit to, too unmanly. But he didn't know Lorraine. She liked men whose woman side was never far from the surface. She loved the tension that crackled just beneath.

As she placed her cheek against his left buttock (her favorite one), she could hear the small animals scrambling through the refuse outside, and the rustle of the trees like a million tiny ponies running on sand.

She grabbed his foot next and pulled him to her. She climbed on top of him and whispered: 'I wish I could fuck you like you fuck me. I wish I could take you the way you take me. I want to climb inside you. Go as deep as I can, Winston.'

He turned his head away. She wasn't sure whether it was out of modesty or out of excitement. Suddenly an overwhelming sadness came over her. She felt sorry for him. Sorry for all men. Men could not surrender. Black men could not surrender. They had surrendered enough.

At least that's the way it seemed to be to her in these days when the brothers dressed in dashikis and climbed atop soapboxes.

If only Winston had been allowed to surrender.

But instead he did what he usually did. He flipped her over on her back, gently pulled her legs open, and entered her with a sound that was a mixture of a sob and a gurgle of joy.

Later, she held him close. He was like a baby. She longed to save him, save him from the streets, from the humiliation he was destined to suffer every day of his life.

She loved his rough kissing. The way the stubble on his chin felt, the taste of his saliva mixed in her mouth, his tongue like a little butterfly fluttering around her face.

He said, 'We're supposed to be dead. We should have died on the Middle Passage, our bones rotting at the bottom of the sea. Baby, have you ever thought how ruthless the ones who made it must have been? How ruthless and blessed? Most folks didn't even survive the trip. Millions died on those ships. At the slave stations on the Coast of Africa, in the bush trying to run away and be free. Can you imagine how *bad* the ones who did survive must have been? The ones who made us?'

It was the summer of 1969. At the end of the year she would be twenty-one years old. Her majority. An official grown woman. An official wise person.

She stopped believing that magic day of escape had ever happened. That there had ever been a Magic Al. Time had caught her, and she had settled in. All she wanted was to be with her man. Time and circumstances were wearing her down. Making her toe the line. Act right.

Lorraine tried to convince herself that being settled was the best thing, even though she knew from African History

Class that she had descended from sub-Saharan hunter-gatherers who scorned those of their people who conformed, who 'put on clothes, work.'

She covered her mouth with her own hand. It was too quiet here for her orgasm. Besides, she had come to cure *him*. Cure him of the pain she saw in his eyes. Take him away from the dangerous, fragile world of black American manhood. They had come up to his parents' summer cabin to get away. They lied when the elders asked how long they'd been married. Lorraine obeyed Winston although she wanted to tell them the truth: they were lovers, but Winston had insisted on a restful weekend. He didn't want to embarrass the old people.

'How come you so crazy?' he laughed when she climbed into the shower with him.

'It's got something to do with going to two churches on Sunday,' she said as she kissed the foam off his back.

Later, he wiped the vapor from the mirror and put her face up to it.

'What do you see?' he asked.

'You.'

'What else?'

'Nothing.'

'You don't want to see what's there. Know what I see? A face like the last good thing that'll ever happen in my life.'

Then he carried her back to bed. In the midst of everything, he allowed her to paint his face. She put all of her make-up on it as carefully and lovingly as she made up her own face. Winston did not resemble a woman so much as a lovely young boy hidden from the world. She kissed the lipstick off his mouth.

They also fought all weekend. And when it was over, and

they had to take the train back down to Chicago, he told her that he had volunteered to go to Vietnam. She slapped his face. She tried to throw his clothing out the window.

She wanted to beat him to death. Kill him before the US Army did.

He left her at Union Station. He did not say goodbye. She stumbled through the canyon that was LaSalle Street. The canyon of steel skyscrapers, of ancient cathedral-like buildings with stained glass windows, of the Stock Exchange with its vulgar-beautiful facade, a tribute to men who knew what they wanted. Men who did not go to war and waste their lives.

She stopped on a bridge overlooking the Chicago River, the river the Irish turned green on St Patrick's Day, the river that ran backwards because rich men wanted it that way. For a moment, she wondered what it would be like to plunge into it, to fall to the bottom among the debris of avarice and conquest. Yes, she would jump, jump overboard from the slave ship of her emotions. She would allow the murky green waters to sweep her to the St Lawrence River and out into the Atlantic and back to where she came from.

She wished that one of those rednecks who called black people up at random and offered passage back to Africa, would suddenly appear on the bridge. She would take him up on it before he could get the words out.

But first she would make him take her for a drink at the Playboy Club. They would enter the cold gray skyscraper on Michigan Avenue, past the gaudy boutique with its Bond Girl saleswomen, and up to the bar. She would demand the redneck order her champagne as her final drink in this wretched city of contradictions. Then off she would go. With her luck she would be dropped off in some place like Biafra where there was a civil war going on.

Just as she got the urge to step over the railing, she saw an old woman. An old woman cursing to herself in the stiff wind. She pulled Lorraine over to where she was standing. 'I keep throwin' pennies in this damn thing, but I still don't get my goddamn wish!'

Something in her voice was like a slap of cold water in Lorraine's face. When she looked around, she saw the entire bridge populated with old black people, some single, some in couples. In the distance an alarm was sounding, but Lorraine did not pay attention to it.

'It's not a fountain,' she said to the old woman, 'it's a river. You're supposed to throw pennies in a fountain, not a river.'

'I'm not puttin' my money in them dirty things. The river's good enough. Come on, child, help me.'

The alarm was louder now. The old black people did not move. Lorraine could not tell whether they were real or not.

The old woman pulled out a coin that looked as old as she was. 'You throw. You young and strong,' the woman urged her. Lorraine threw the coin as far as she could. 'Yeah,' the woman said, 'I see it. You goin' far. Far away. Far. Don't throw yourself off this bridge. Not yet. You got too far to go. Your daddy's still around. His eyes are gettin' darker, he can barely see anything at all. That's 'cause his eyes are full of your face.'

Now there was a great shimmer around the old woman. Lorraine knew who She was.

So she bowed her head and the Old Woman touched it in a kind of benediction. When Lorraine raised her head, the Old Woman had vanished and in her place stood a yelling, red-faced white man.

'Lady, you deaf! Can't you hear that alarm! The bridge is

goin' up, a big ship's comin' through from the St Lawrence Seaway. You wanna get killed?'

He yanked her off the bridge and into the throng that watched the big ship sail beneath the raised bridge. She did not ask him if he had seen the old woman, or if he had seen any of the old people on the bridge.

She knew he hadn't.

Lorraine slowly opened the file with her name on it. Every stricture that she had ever learned from both her mother and the nuns came flooding back to her. What had Sister Calixta said about stealing? That it was an abomination to God, even a mortal sin in some cases. And her mother? 'If thy hand offend thee . . .'

'Now's your chance to see what that white boy's been sayin' about us,' Winston said as he rifled the rest of the file cabinet in the Dean's office.

Lorraine had never thought of Dean Murray as a 'white boy.' He didn't seem to be human at all, but a creature from another planet. He was attempting to grow his crew cut out, even though he looked the other way when some of the girls danced topless on the lawn between classes.

She could hear his tentative voice now on the phone in the next room trying to remain calm as he told his wife that he would not be home for dinner. 'What if he sees us?' Lorraine asked, indicating the open door and the Dean sitting at his desk, the glare from the overhead light bouncing off his bald spot.

'So what?', Winston shot back as he pulled out his own file, 'I'm not goin' to the 'Nam 'till I discuss this one comment here right now.' He grabbed his file. 'Fuck it.'

Sit-ins were too strenuous, even for good causes. Professor

McClaren, who had invited her over for tea, had already agreed to set up several African Studies Courses anyway.

When Winston and the other brothers marched into McClaren's office demanding he do just that, he readily agreed, then insisted that they all sit down and listen to the nuances in the Jimi Hendrix record he was blasting in his back room. In fact, McClaren helped them stage the sit-in himself, and was outside acting as a kind of Information Officer. He was having a great time. He smoked a joint with her off-campus, and gave her a bracelet he had brought back from Kenya.

'You don't mind a white boy giving this to you?' he asked, 'I mean, I know it's not righteous.' He spoke with a kind of swing to his head. 'You know, Lorraine, there's quite a lot I could teach you. I'm going to Washington on a march. I've got some friends in Virginia. Would you like to come with me? We could stay with them. I want to introduce you to the music of Cat Stevens. A great romantic. Like me.'

Lorraine gingerly opened her own manila folder in the Dean's office. She cringed when she saw the photo she had taken in her freshman year with the Diana Ross hair-do and Ronnie Spector eye make-up. There she was. Off to college with stacks and stacks of fashion magazines, required reading in her last year at highschool. She was going to college, she had to get everything right. The black girls there had their own sororities and other organizations but she intended to join the other ones, too, because she had to experience everything.

She and Lana had been like a black Sandra Dee and Annette Funicello then, giggly and anxious. It had all been so important then.

That importance lasted one year. After one year, Lorraine gave up her bi-weekly trip to the hairdresser to achieve the

Motown Look. Instead she let her hair, in the disgusted expression of her former hairdresser whom she ran into once downtown, 'revert.' When Elvira saw her she was furious. But she didn't care. She gave away all of her smart fashion magazine clothing. There were to be no more parties, activities, weekend trips, teas, shopping sprees or the other flotsam and jetsam of black campus society.

She chose, instead, to live in the 'Black House,' where authentic 'African' cuisine and not so authentic 'African' customs were observed. Students changed their names to the annoyance of the university registrar and the fury of their parents. They no longer wanted to be known by their 'slave names' but by names of their own choosing. Names which reflected the dream of a millennial Mother Africa.

Lorraine toyed for a while with the idea of changing hers. But all of the names somehow seemed false, and funny, too. She just couldn't reconcile some of the majestic titles now carried by former super-cool 'freshies' whose main concern had been the state of their Mustangs, T-Birds, and Brooks Brothers pullovers.

She really thought that things had gotten out of hand when, the morning after a one-night-stand with a Chinese sax player who said that he often communed with Coltrane in his dreams, he announced to her that he had once been a Black Muslim, but had been thrown out because he wouldn't change his name.

'You know,' he said as he pulled on his shirt quietly so as not to wake her roommate, 'they wanted me to be George Twenty X. I said my name wasn't no slave name. My name is CHEN. That name is thousands of years old, baby! But they couldn't hear me. I messed up their programme. So I had to split.'

They liked jazz in the Black House, but not the blues. The blues was considered the music of an oppressed people best left to those with a taste for nostalgia, and white students who found their own culture bankrupt.

Soul, largely rooted in gospel music, was preferred with its implication of triumph over the Devil.

So, for a brief time, Lorraine put aside her father's records in exchange for the 'gloria in excelsis' of Marvin Gaye and Tammi Terrell, the apocalyptic yearning in the songs of the Four Tops, Stevie Wonder's celebration of the power and the glory of black urban life, Jimi Hendrix's iconoclastic rewrite of the definition of the black experience, the 'Natural Woman' in the voice of Aretha Franklin and Martha Reeves.

Aretha's voice had the same quality of purity and belief that Lorraine found at Mass. It did not have the undertone of Bessie Smith's, with its disbelief in the future. The future implied a benevolence that did not exist. But Aretha was from the church. The world of Lorraine's mother. Soul implied a life beyond the present, whether it was in heaven or down on earth. The blues was not welcome. The baby-boomers were not interested in life as it really was.

For a time, neither was Lorraine. She was tired of being different, tired of asking questions no one else asked, tired of being left out of the great mass of those who were convinced of the rightness of their lives.

Yet she just couldn't accept things like everyone else did. There were too many questions with too few answers.

What part did her people play in their own oppression? And if she was part of her people could she be something more? Was there something more?

Lorraine thought all this as she tore her Diana Ross picture up into confetti-like pieces. She dug deeper into the file. It was all there: her refusal to take the pledge of allegiance when a general, fresh from combat in Vietnam, had come to address the school; the afternoon she had danced topless to 'The Doors' in a local hang-out after passing her exams.

But with the exception of the Diana Ross picture she liked her file. She was fascinated by her slide into perdition which seemed to have accelerated as time went on.

Just as she closed the file, Bernard ran up to her, breathless, the Black Panther symbol and the Vietcong flag both securely pinned to his right breast. 'Hey, it's time to go,' he sputtered.

'Go where?' Lorraine demanded. 'We can't go anywhere. This is a sit-in!'

'Fuck that! We got tickets for *Hair*!'

She'd forgotten that this was the night they had planned to go downtown to see the musical. She carefully put her file back in place, unlike the other students who were busy photocopying theirs, and followed Bernard down the back staircase. The hall was patrolled by an elite guard of black and white men recruited from the ROTC who were risking their scholarships and future Army commissions by taking part in the protest.

Outside, radical white students were making speeches in solidarity. Megaphones were everywhere. How would she and Bernard explain leaving the building at a time like this, especially to see a theatrical representation of what was taking place in real life?

'Dig,' Bernard said as they walked past a Weatherman in a faded Army jacket who eyed them suspiciously. 'If we're stopped, we're just going out to get supplies. That's what they say in the cowboy movies, right? Or if it's one of them Weathermen, we just jump bad and ask them why they ques-

tionin' black folks. "If you not part of the solution, you part
of the problem, etc." We can do it, Lorraine.'

Lorraine remembered, as they boarded a subway train
bound for the Loop, that she hadn't taken a bath in two
days. She remembered because a black woman sucked her
teeth as she passed. The woman, her hair done up in tight,
greasy, over-straightened curls, had a copy of the Bible on
her lap. She was like the women who attended her mother's
church. Good sisters who brooked no nonsense.

The campus disappeared below as the train roared into the
city. A drunk rolled up, watching them for some time. He
had yellow eyes and wore a 'Chicago Cubs' sweatshirt underneath what looked as if it had once been an undertaker's suit.

The woman began furiously to leaf through her Bible. The
pages were old and fragile, dried roses served as bookmarks.
The dried roses made her seem more delicate, vulnerable to
the exigencies of this world. Bernard paid no attention
to either of them. He was much too busy singing the score
of *Hair* which he had studied relentlessly every night. He was
determined to be on stage at the finale.

A youth gang plunged through the doors, fighting their
way though the car as the train rattled on the ancient tracks
high above tenements that had once been elegant mansions
on tree-lined avenues. The gang stopped for a moment and
gave them the peace sign, then resumed fighting their way
to the next car. The woman started a chorus of 'What a
Friend we Have in Jesus.' Lorraine was amazed at the power
that emanated from her frail body.

During her time at the Black House, she had studied the
Yoruba pantheon. To her the woman with the Bible, with
her sturdy air, was Yemoja the mother, queen of the goddesses.
And the drunken man with his piercing eyes, could be none

other than Elegba, the trickster, the Guardian-at-the-Threshold, the Devil-at-the-Crossroads, the blues itself. She knew him. She knew him because Elegba was always summoning her, too. He always showed up to remind her that she had a journey to take. That she was just passing through.

The drunk leaned closer to them. His face was the color of night, as full of crevices as the side of a mountain. His fingers were long, the fingers of a pianist, Lorraine thought. The woman stopped singing and pushed him along with her newspaper. He moved away and put his face right up to Lorraine's. Bernard nervously rearranged the fringe jacket he was wearing. The drunk, washing their faces in the fumes of his breath, said: 'What y'all supposed to be? Hippies?'

Lorraine could barely keep Bernard in his seat during the show. When the 'White Boys' number started he sank down in surprise and disgust. 'Girl, look up there. Do you know who that is?' he hissed. 'That's Anna-Mae Bowie! You remember her. Her daddy raised her after her mama left. She used to wear mix-match socks to school, and her panties were never clean. Look up on that stage. I'll be damned! That's her! I wonder what that bitch is calling herself now.'

Anna-Mae. Always trying to please, always trying to get people to love her. Anna-Mae even sat through two Masses during Lent. It was rumored once that she was going to be a nun. Then she got into trouble with a Puerto Rican boy, the handsomest boy in school. Some said she had an abortion, even at the young age of thirteen. Then she moved away.

Lorraine looked through her programme. Anna-Mae was now known as 'Josette, actress' ('I owe it all to my Mississippi grandmother,' her biog. read).

Anna-Mae shook her Afro and wiggled her way through the song. Anna-Mae's piety had merely been a form of exhibitionism after all. She was, in a manner of speaking, once more in church. There was a 'congregation' present to impress with her fervor. When the cast appeared nude in the finale, Bernard whispered as if he were in church: 'I'm going to be in that show. And then go to Europe. If that tack-head can do it, I can do it. I'm gettin' the hell outta Dodge!'

Bernard took the book out of her hand and placed it next to him. The sun was shining in her eyes so that she could barely see. She put her hand up to his face. He took it and kissed it. 'Don't worry about McClaren's exam,' he said. 'He's stoned all the time anyway. He'll pass us. He don't want to be a bad honky.'

She wasn't worried about McClaren's exam. She'd already taken it and passed, in a manner of speaking, but she listened dutifully to Bernard anyway. He was a well-meaning person.

She closed the book and lay back on the grass. It was the kind of spring day where the air was light and strong. She rolled over and put her head in his lap. She felt the heat from his thighs.

'So, how about it?' she asked.

Bernard stroked her hair. 'You're Winston's lady,' he answered.

'I'm my own lady,' she said, even though she knew what she was saying was a lie.

'Nope,' he said, 'I don't need the brother to come down on me.'

The other black students were huddled around a guest speaker, a field recruiter for the Southern Christian Leadership Conference. It was only a year after Dr King had been assassinated. No one wanted to talk about non-violence. Some of the students were walking away to watch an impromptu basketball game that had formed in the middle of the speaker's talk.

'I just want you to take me to the dance,' Lorraine said to Bernard. She suddenly felt like a character out of a Walt Disney movie. This coy, coquettish pose did not suit her, but everything else she had ever tried with Bernard failed. And it was necessary today not to feel like a failure.

A white student walked past and waved. 'They always think you want to be with them,' Bernard muttered as he waved back. Then suddenly he said, 'I know.'

'You know what?'

'OK, I know about Lana. She told me she was pregnant. I know it's Winston's. I didn't want to come down on him because he's my frat brother. I knew about you and her. Winston was dealin' with both of you. I knew. Brother man had some very busy nights. I'm sorry, Lorraine. But you can't use me to front him off.'

Something crashed inside Lorraine. She felt old.

The white student seemed to be coming back toward them. He wore a flower over his left earlobe. Bernard pulled her up and they hurried over to the spot where the black students were meeting. 'Sit down, brother and sis, I'd like to talk to you,' the recruiter said when they came over. They sat down, more to discourage the white student from joining them than anything else. The recruiter's full Afro formed a halo around his face. It made him look like a beautiful saint.

'OK, I know you think the time has passed for non-violence,' he said. 'I understand what you sayin'. I've been trained in non-violence, I've had the shit kicked out of me, shit dumped on me, so I know what I'm talkin' about. You don't have to be no saint. Many a night I lay up in my bed wantin' to kill, but I didn't 'cause in the end I knew that that wouldn't free us.

'The day Dr King was killed, I was ready to take myself over to the Lorraine Motel where he died . . . Yeah I was in Memphis to help with the garbage strike . . . I was ready to go on over to the Lorraine Motel and shoot the goddamn place up. But all my years of training taught me that's no good, 'cause in the end you got to pay. So I know. I know, that in the end, might will not prevail. We can't win a fight with might.'

'Hey, man, you crazy! Let's separate from these mutha-fuckas!,' someone in the gathering shouted. 'Let's have our own country! We worked that land down south, we're the proletariat. Fuck tryin' to get along with this monster. There ain't no gettin' along with it. It's Toms like you that play into the hands of those who want to destroy us. Comin' here talkin' about non-violence. Non-violence! Don't nothin' in the animal kingdom turn the other cheek but niggers! I'm tired of havin' the moral advantage. I want some real advantage.'

Most of the students applauded. The recruiter adjusted his glasses and stood up. 'Peace. Thank-you for your time,' he said as he walked away. 'Peace.' How could there be peace? Lorraine felt her belly. She too had been pregnant by Winston, only a few days ago, and now Lana. Lana, her best friend.

Her belly was slowly going down as a result of the abortion. She was surprised that she felt such loss, such emptiness. She felt loss and the emptiness in the recruiter, too. She followed him down the hill.

She walked behind him at a discreet distance. She followed him into a bar off campus. On the jukebox Dinah Washington, 'Queen of the Blues,' was singing 'Blue Gardenia.' The music seemed to come not from the jukebox, but from the afternoon itself, to issue forth from the street, from the very earth low and sweet. The earth where there was peace.

The recruiter was already drinking. ' "Jack Daniels" and soda?,' he asked her without looking up. She nodded, although she had never had it before. They drank in silence. The sun streamed into the doorway, bathing the old Polish men in the corner in a red glow, as if they were drinking in pools of blood.

'Times sure have changed, right pops?' the recruiter said as he raised his drink to one of the men. The man did not blink an eye. He sat as if no one was speaking to him.

'You kids are all fired up,' the recruiter said to her abruptly. 'Can't blame you. Just the other day, I was walkin' down some red dirt road in Georgia thinkin' murderous thoughts. Murderous thinkin' runs in my family. My daddy spent some time on the chain gang with Leadbelly. They took my father away because he talked too much. So I decided to spend my life doin' nothin' but talkin', and I have succeeded. But you kids today, you don't want to hear no talk. None at all. And that I can understand.'

Suddenly something in Lorraine made her say, 'That's not the way you speak. You talk that way so people won't be intimidated by you.'

The recruiter laughed. 'Very perceptive. *In vino veritas.*'

They walked in the cool evening air, she empty and carved out, he empty and carved out. Drowning in their whiskey-peace.

'Sometimes,' he said, 'I go out to the Georgia Sea Islands where my grandmama lives, or go walking down by the creek my daddy used to fish. For the peace. Just be a fisherman, or a painter, or a drunk. Or a lover. Nothing special. Nothing dramatic. I go from place to place. I don't understand why.

Used to blame it on my mama. Once a week she'd hop a freight and go somewhere. Her territory, she'd say, but I think she went for the hell of it. Daddy would've gone, too, if that had been considered decent. And, let me tell you, decency was his *raison d'être*. My mama lost her leg, I found out later, hopping freights. Didn't stop her. She kept on moving. I went looking for her once after she was gone for two months. I think I set out to kill her. I never found her. Lost. Loss. My father named me "Marion". He said he didn't want to bring another black man into this world.'

She drank with him until the sun went down. Then he took her to a place to eat that she had never heard of before. They drank good Scotch, ate chicken fried steak, mashed potatoes, and greens. He ordered a large slice of peach cobbler which he helped her eat. They went to a club on a sidestreet to hear the blues queen Koko Taylor, Koko with her wide stance, bellowing 'I'm a Woman,' her answer to Muddy Waters' 'I'm a Man.'

At one point, when she had been dancing in the aisles with practically everyone in the room, Marion asked her name. 'Lorraine,' she called out.

'Say, Lorraine,' he said, 'remind me to tell you something later on.'

He took her back to his one-room flat, the type known as 'kitchenettes' which Dr King had come to Chicago two years earlier to condemn. There was clothing scattered around and empty bottles. Several photos of Dr King were spread out on the small table. The picture of a young woman dressed in the baggy farmer's jeans known as 'Freedom Overalls' lay on the table beside his bed. Lorraine heard a man next door through the thin walls coughing and farting. The smell of greasy cooking wafted under the door.

Marion made no effort to clean up the room. Instead, he perched on the edge of his bed and pulled out a Harmonica. 'Are you familiar with the blues? Sonny Boy Williamson?'

'Which one? The first or the second?' she replied. He howled in delight at her knowledge. Then he played his harmonica. 'What's that'? she asked. ' "Eyesight To the Blind" by Sonny Boy II.'

She sang with Marion. They sang until the cooking smells faded into the night, and the man next door was long asleep. They sang until the light came up.

And when the light came up she told him about the abortion, and that she was still bleeding from it, and then she cried and he held her. She climbed into his bed just as the street came alive. She came to his bed with the words of the nuns, the words of her mother ringing in her ear. Her mother standing at her pulpit in her great robes, exhorting all within the sound of her voice to give themselves to the understanding that the world was shaped by Will and the great love of God. All that it took was surrender. All that it took was belief.

'Do you know something,' he said to her as they lay in the pool of the noonday sun that spilled onto his bed, 'I don't think a blues person, something more than an aficionado I mean, ever stays still. They just roam the world, looking for more blues. Somewhere in their heart they try to settle down. But it's no use. The blues has come down on them. And when that happens you see something but it may take you a long time to know what you see.'

And she did remember what Marion had said (although she did not understand it), when, while home for her birthday, the telephone rang.

She took off her Prince Charles badge and as she was walking past the extension, she accidentally heard the voice on the other end. A voice from so long ago that it seemed to come from another world.

Her father.

She picked it up.

'Daddy?'

For a moment there was dead silence on the other end. As if the entire world had stopped. Then she heard his voice again, the voice she sometimes heard when she was not listening to anything at all.

'Lorraine, baby?'

'Daddy? Is that you? I thought . . . Where are you?'

'In New York City darlin' I just thought I'd call up to say "Hi" It's your birthday your mama says she was givin' you a party you got a man friend huh? your mama says he seems nice that's good your birthday how could I forget that? yeah I can remember that day like I remember hittin' that beach at D-Day On the day you were born there was a little snow fallin' down hawk blowin' like crazy your mama huffin' and puffin' tryin' to get you born 'cause that Prince Charlie was on his way and you know how your mama loves competition you came but too early I told her that was the way you were goin' to be in life if she didn't watch out ahead of everybody was I right child? baby between you and me I think your mama is workin' too hard too hard God's work is for God not human beings watch her . . .'

He was talking like a used car salesman. She couldn't stop him.

'Daddy, where . . .'

'Shoot I'm runnin' out of money I sing about you I sing about you on the corners or in the doorways when it rains'

And then the phone went dead.

She closed her eyes, and when she opened them, Elvira was standing there.

'Mama . . . you knew he was alive all the time.'

'Yes, baby.'

'Why didn't you . . .?'

'Because, darlin'. Because. I knew him before you did. He belonged to me first. Lorraine, you promised me. Not before you're thirty. Not before God's time.'

The room whirled and suddenly went dark. In the darkness Lorraine could see her mother and father, dressed in their bridal clothes, walking down a flower-strewn path past her, their child, a floating corpse in a dead sea.

When she opened her eyes, Elvira was sitting beside her reading quietly from the Bible. Lorraine closed her eyes again. She understood.

The conspiracy that had been going on all these years was a kind of love. The terrible burden of love. And she must not intrude.

She would wait until she was thirty.

Then she would go to New York and find him.

She left for New York on the day of her thirtieth birthday, in the middle of a blizzard. As she drove away, she looked back to catch a last glimpse of her mother.

But Elvira had vanished, swallowed up in the swirling snow.

judgements are the fathers of their garments

1984. The dreaded year. The one they always warned about. So far the only terrible thing that happened was the Ronald Reagan Film Festival on late-night TV. That knocked out television since Lorraine had a strange set that could only pick up one channel. She could always sit out on the fire escape and listen to the junkies on the roof regale one another with fantastic tales. After all, wasn't New York a festival of choice?

She could always go down to Brooklyn where Lana, now known as Sister Rashid, ran an African Health Centre, where she offered healing to stressed out black Wall Street executives and other high flyers who wanted to maintain their cultural identity and still participate in the smash and grab culture that had become a way of life in New York.

Only the other Saturday, Lorraine had participated in a ritual bath for an insurance executive who was making $100,000 a year and found he could no longer eat fried chicken. It gave him bad memories, and confused him to the point of collapse.

Sister Rashid counseled him, had him undress and Lorraine then took over. She led him into a steamy bath fragrant with exotic herbs, and with Billie Holiday on the cassette outside the door, Lorraine scrubbed him raw with an 'African brush.'

It was easy money. She had to stay in New York somehow.

This was a far cry from the day she and Lana left Chicago together.

Elvira had gathered what seemed like the entire congregation to see them off. Lorraine assured her mother that she was not blasting into outer space, only going to live nine hundred miles away. She had waited until she was thirty as she promised. She had worked forty different jobs so that she wouldn't have to tie herself down to anything. Now it was time to go.

Lana had brought along her ex-boyfriend Gary to help with the driving. Gary was in his early twenties and believed that black men were the wretched of the earth. This was mainly due to black women.

He talked about it a lot on the trip.

He also began snorting cocaine as soon as her mother and the congregation were out of sight. Lorraine thought there would be room for her in the car, but Lana had brought along, in addition to all her clothing, four rather large fur coats she was planning to sell in New York.

The snow in both senses died out as they were driving across Pennsylvania. They pulled into a diner at five in the morning and Gary began trying to talk to the waitress, a dyed blonde with too much eyeliner. It was like a scene out of a bad movie.

Lorraine looked for the exit as five white hunters came in with their rifles crooked over their arms. Gary began to challenge them. Lana tried to pull him away. That was when he went into his tirade about black women.

Lorraine prayed that they would reach New York alive.

When they drove into the Bronx, Lorraine could barely see from lack of sleep. They headed for the address Lana had.

The building was barely a shell, but there were people living there. Lana disappeared inside, and Gary went to score, talking at the top of his lungs in his broad Midwestern accent.

There were burnt-out buildings that had windows painted on tin coverings. From the elevated train roaring past they must have looked like the real thing, a reassuring sight for the Long Island commuter.

The streets were tight and dirty, but there was something thrilling about the closeness, the thuggishness of it. Chicago had been like a small village compared to this. It was just like it was in the movies. Yes, she would find her father here.

Gary never returned so Lana drove her down to the Village. They were both amazed at how the streets went up and down because Chicago was on the prairie and flat. They found her friend Tommy's house, a Village brownstone with Village character.

He was cooking spaghetti and trying on women's wigs when she arrived. Lana did not stay. Tommy hugged her and promptly offered her a tab of acid that he had bought at the foot of the Pyramids. He had secured her a job packing Christmas candy and she was to start tomorrow. But meantime, they were to spend their time getting high.

She remembered a little of the day: that they had ridden in a carriage through Central Park singing Cole Porter songs; how they wound up in the Metropolitan Museum Of Art and how she kept remarking on how she had seen all the paintings before in her school books. They wound up at Grand Central Station in rush hour. They joined the hurrying crowds. They thought everyone was rushing to a party. They were from Chicago. They were not about to miss a party.

But all of that seemed so long ago now, when she was still

a black girl from the Midwest hoping for a miracle.

Now she was simply tired and lonely and there for the sake of being there. And tonight the Black Women's Caucus was going to separate from the Women's Group.

Just the other day she sat in on one of the longest meetings in her life while the Black Women's Caucus went over their grievances. Over and over and over. She had fallen asleep more than once.

Joining the group was Sister Rashid's idea. She told Lorraine over cups of mu-tea that she had lost touch with her roots because of her haphazard relationships with men, and her lack of female friends. Lorraine was too bored to disagree.

Besides, Lana had always had a taste for the extreme gesture, the massive comment. It was just that Lorraine couldn't be bothered to tell her that she just didn't want to be another 'sister.'

Now tonight. It wasn't until she had to restrain herself from laughing at Sasha Dubchek's owl-glasses and earnest voice that she realized she might be drunk. She blocked out the voice as best she could, as she found a place at the back where the black women were glowering in silent fury.

Sasha began the proceedings. This was unfortunate. The vodka was swirling round in Lorraine's head. She closed her eyes to try to stop it. Someone was talking. It sounded like her voice, the voice of a drunk woman muttering to herself.

'Now what in the hell am I doing here? I've got a stew to make back home . . . I mean I have a recipe to read about a stew . . . No, I don't need to put that much meat in it. Meat is bad. They say meat kills you. Rashid says that soul food was the shit they gave us to eat. Soul food is a conspiracy. Black folks eat too much soul food which really has nothing to do with our souls. But it damn sure has to do with *their* wallets. *Them*. White folks always manage to creep in some-where. Statement: "Yeah, I stepped in some dog shit in the street." Response: "How come the streets aren't clean? The white man only keeps his section straight." Statement: "It looks like rain." Response: "That's what the white man says. How long is it goin' to take before you stop believing him." Why am I talking like this? I sound like Lana, I mean Sister Rashid. I can't stand these African names. Why do black women have such strange names? 'Cause we couldn't name ourselves for so long ... excuses, excuses. Black folks think those names are grand. Lord, am I glad that Mama didn't name me something like Chalandra Annette Williams. Then I'd get married and become Chalandra Annette Williams hyphen something. I hate those hyphens. Nobody has hyphens except English aristocratic families. Oh yeah, we're claiming it now ... Ugh. I sound like those backlash bitches at the insurance company who say if it was left to women we'd still be in mud huts. Yeah, well maybe mud huts ain't so bad compared to vapor, which we will be if they keep messing around with all these nuclear weapons. If they drop one on New York just give me five minutes so I can go running toward Times Square. Then I'll be vaporized on a wall. A wall print. A shadow. A real spook ... What's Sasha doing? Scratching her crotch. She wears the same girdle I wear, I saw her buy it. She didn't see me. I was slapping some paint on some African chieftain's wife's face when in came Sasha and she bought my girdle ... Why doesn't Sasha admit she's Jewish? She is Jewish. What's she scared of these days? At least she'll have the consolation if she's mugged, she's mugged as a white person. History does have its rewards ... Ssh, stop talking. Those days are over. Nobody cares about women's organizations. Nobody cares about women ... I like

Jews. Yeah, it's true. Especially nice Jewish boys. They'll do anything. Asking a brother to go down on you is like asking him to talk against his mama . . . What was it that brother said to me last night about black men getting down on their knees . . . "no way, that's degrading . . ." And they want to know why Polly wants a cracker? 'Course I don't have the courage to be a dyke . . . they always find me out anyway . . . I'm a traitor, an intellectual lesbian, a professional black woman whose job is being black in certain situations that benefit her . . . fuck the race . . . and dykes and niggers always find me out . . . they ain't stupid . . . they don't need me . . . people like me . . . the fucked-up ones . . . the one in the back with the little question to ask after everybody else is shouting with their fists raised . . . I slow shit down . . . black women like me slow shit down . . . I can sleep with a woman but I'm not into them . . . be black, but what is that . . . I've read too many Jewish philosophers . . . Stop this . . . I am not anti-Semitic. Too scared, too bored, too tired to be anti-anything . . . We are not intellectual beings, we are sensate beings. Our senses, our petty prejudices, our fear of an alien smell, an alien skin defeats our brain . . . One of the sisters is talking about Jewish women . . . oh, not that again . . . The 'Sistuhs' hate Jews 'cause they hated their teachers . . . This is revenge on all their schoolteachers who made them take the day off on Rosh Hoshana, but fuck Malcolm X's birthday . . . he wasn't even dead then, I don't mean him . . . Marcus Garvey, DuBois . . . you know what I mean . . . They should have had nuns . . . nuns weren't humans, Jews are, so they do things like have holidays and they're upfront about it. They don't talk about heaven, they're now, and black people like heaven, and Jews aren't into heaven . . . that's it, that's the philosophical nub of it . . . yes, I ought to point that out to them . . . the 'Sistuhs' . . . they're nice girls . . . I can help them think, think about what they are saying right now . . . think it through as I've thought it through . . . but we aren't intellectual beings we are . . . Who am I talkin' like . . . "as I've thought it through?" . . . Stand up and . . . can't stand very well now . . . I mean, I can but I can't stand still. Got to keep moving . . . move on . . . to every blues joint in town . . . no dad . . . what do I think he's goin' to do anyway when I see his face? . . . Yeah, he got something to say to me . . . some fatherly wisdom . . . oops, I better be quiet . . . daddys are bad guys around here . . . AMONG THE WOMEN!!! . . . but we're tired. We outnumber men, why do we have to take all this shit off them? Everything is he, he, he . . . we're the majority . . . it's the 'y' chromosome . . . it's defective . . . say, we can create something that stops the mutation in the womb . . . the 'Y' mutation . . . we have to . . . because they'll kill us . . . they are killing us . . . Oswald Williams, my father . . . yeah, I can see it . . . he'll walk right up to me, and just wipe away the years . . . right . . . no, that's a song . . . who sung that . . . somebody sung that . . . but he will . . . I know he will . . . I hope he will because I need him to tell me . . . what I am living for . . . he knows why . . . he'll tell me . . . that's his job . . . tell me . . . where is he? . . . Give me back my face. I can't even see myself in the mirror, man . . . give me . . . oops, what's goin' on now . . . Sasha's crying. She's got pretty eyes. Very long black lashes. I think she's been trying to come on to me. Or maybe I've been trying to come on to her. Hard to say right at this very moment in time . . . Too much booze. Mama would not approve. Would Daddy? . . . There's one more place I haven't gone to. I'll just stand in the middle of Times Square all day. I'll stand there and wait for Oswald Williams to show up . . .

I'm glad I'm not a man. It is not a man's world . . . I have nothing against women. That time Karen and I did it was nice. But she's too squishy . . . Women are squishy. I don't like squishy. I like hard. I like very hard. I don't want my life story to be about sisters. There're too many sisters. Sisters are everywhere. How'd we get to be everywhere? . . . I wonder what it must be like for men . . . This is 1984. Big Brother is Little Brother and shrinking fast. It's about time . . . They've had enough, now they should move over and let us drive. A good slogan. "Let us drive." I know all the words to the Mickey Mouse Club song; "Today is Monday, you know what that means . . ." They must be shit-scared. Men. I'd be shit-scared if I was a man. Three-legs. One of these sisters calls them three-legs. Hooray for the three legs! . . . What? What are they sayin'? . . . I've heard all this before . . . Who's that? Yeah, that's Carmen. Carmen's the one in the middle. She's got a black mother and white father. They met at Selma in the sixties or something weird like that . . . I remember Selma! I've got a past! Yippee! What am I cheering about? I'm living past my time. Whole goddamn generation living past its time . . . I wish I had another vodka. I'd like to go where they grow vodka except that's Russia, shit no, it's too cold there. But we could all learn something from the Russians. We could all learn to drink vodka . . . I am a drunk. Admit it, girl. How did that happen to you? A woman is not supposed to be a drunk. Noooooo. A black woman is supposed to go to church. Keep her dignity. Uphold the race. Blah, blah, blah . . . Poor Mama with a daughter like me. What will happen to the Tabernacle when she dies? I don't have an obligation to that. I have an obligation to me. I think. That's the new code now . . . Me. Me . . . Tried to stand up for me yesterday in the office when O'Brian called me in to ask about my writing on the files. He can't understand how I write. That's racist . . . Hmm, maybe he's right. My writing has deteriorated, all due to the little nips I have at home at night, and before I go to bed, and when I wake up, and on coffee breaks . . . Can't read my writing! See, black people have a way of writing. We have our own language, too . . . They ought to pay us reparations like they paid the Indians. Forty acres and a mule, they owe us that shit. They took us out of where we were, messed us up, now THEY complain. PAY UP MOTHERFUCKER! I can't say that word. That word denigrates . . . I sound stupid . . .

'Why do almost all the nasty words have to do with women? Why is a weak man a pussy? Why is a pussy a pussy? Mama never gave me any sex education. She wanted me to be a preacher. Preachers don't have sex. Preachers preach . . . This is a country of preachers. Religion is everything. We have freedom of worship. That makes everybody obsessed with God . . . Stopped thinking about God because He's not thinking about me. I can prove it. I went to Bloomingdale's for the sale and my favorite dress, the only dress in the whole world that made me look slim, the one I *prayed* for is G-O-N-E. So there is no God . . . Could there be a Goddess? There is a Goddess. No there isn't. I mean there is, but just why do they think she's not in business any more. Because she was a bitch! She fucked over people! The men took her out! They got hip to the fact that they had something to do with making babies . . . Oh, what the nuns would think now. I know they would think I'm talking about God as if I'm on infinite (or do I mean intimate) terms, with the almighty . . . Now what's happening? Let me get my purse. The sisters are moving out . . . Round 'em up! Move 'em in, move 'em out Rawhide! I'm outta here! I'm walking out, too. I have to. I'm a sister. Right on! . . . I'm walking down the stairs and out onto the street. Yep, I guess we have walked out. We have joined the great mass of black people who have walked out of lots of things, or been denied access, or been kicked out. We are now separatists. We have now separated ourselves from whatever we were attached to and now we are on our way to our separate black existences as we continue to live in the white man's world. We just take it and make it afro-centered. Yippee! We just claim that everything good was stolen from *us*. We invented everything! If it was good, it started in Africa. That's right . . . I'm going to tell this bum right here on the street just that very fact, but I don't think he can understand me just right now. He's got some wine to drink. Never mind. One monkey don't stop no show. We will triumph someday as soon . . . as we make lots of money. As soon as we can go back to Africa with lots of money and plenty of hair products everything will be alright. Like a Walt Disney movie. We go to the Mother Country and announce: "Oh yoo-oo." Here we are, the black Americans come back home. We got stolen away but we're back and by the way, there's going to be a golden age . . . Those Africans must think we're crazy. I need another drink because I know where I'm going there will be nothing to drink. Half of these women are Muslims and they don't drink. I don't mess with that . . . Ronald Reagan. His America is based on that stupid movie *King's Row*. It's not stupid. It's mighty. It's changing this country. I've seen it ten times. Why have I seen *Kings Row* ten times? The only black person in that movie was the maid who had one line. Probably had a PhD, too, in real life. Oh yeah and there was a statue, too, of a black jockey on the gate where the sign says "King's Row. A good town." . . . What's happening!! I'm being put in a cab. Hey, wait. The cab driver doesn't speak English. The sisters are all outside waving goodbye. Eek, this is the coach to Castle Dracula . . . Look at the sisters. They don't look happy. Come on back for a drink, my sisters. Lighten up. It's an old struggle. You say that's precisely the point. That's why I'm not at their caucus meeting . . . Because I'm too drunk and a bad example, and it's too old a struggle to blow it with someone like me . . . "Hope I die before I get old. Talkin' 'bout my g..g..generation!" . . . My father would approve. My bluesman father would shake my hand. I struck out for freedom. Freedom. I haven't found nothing but this itch. This itch to keep moving. To keep going . . . Daddy where are you? You would have the answers. I'm too old for this. I'm almost thirty-six years old, I better have the answers by now . . . I want to check my face in this cab driver man's mirror. But there's no face to see. I couldn't take anymore excitement . . . He got me home. The man who can't speak English got me home. If you can call it home . . . Manuel sits out front with a machete on his lap. He wheezes all the time. It's too cold here for Puerto Ricans. New York is too cold for anybody . . . I love this light-switch in the hallway. This old, fucked up, light-switch. From the *belle époque*. I know that era. I studied it. I went to a good school. Mama worked hard so I could go there . . . To bed alone. To bed alone. I am not going over to Tommy's to help him tonight. I don't need money that bad. I mean, the nuns didn't teach me to sit astride a man's lap while he takes a dump. Even for $50 . . . Let me check out this mirror one more time. Right. Nothing. Just checking . . . good night!'

Lorraine lay silently, listening to the street below. It was strangely quiet, as if the world were holding its breath. Something had shifted. She felt it. She could always feel these things. It was a knack that people who waited had.

She woke in the middle of the night. She checked the answer-phone which she had been too drunk to check earlier.

There was a message from home. Elvira was dying. She had to return at once.

Lorraine closed her eyes. She liked the sweet spinning of her head, the alcohol dancing in her brain. It was numbing. It was good. It was like a merry-go-round that helped her go to sleep.

She whispered goodbye to New York. She knew that when she left this time, she would not return.

And she was right.

It took Elvira two years to die.

In The White Room
Chicago 1986

'. . . and though, besides all this, whiteness has even been made significant of gladness, for among the Romans a white stone marked a joyful day . . .'

Lorraine heard Moby D's voice once again as she went into Elvira's room. The voice of Moby D, the black prophet of whiteness, rang through the room as she approached her mother's bed.

Elvira's room was completely white. It was as if her mother, her once powerful mother, was adrift on a sea of white, floating precariously on top of the waves of her illness. Elvira was a female Robinson Crusoe, washed ashore in the tatters and rags of her life. But there was no Friday to guide her. No Friday to keep her alive.

Lorraine touched her mother's head. She had never

touched her mother's head before. Elvira opened her eyes and smiled the smile of a child. Her eyes were very large and clear. She did not know who Lorraine was. She raised her right hand and placed it on Lorraine's cheek. Lorraine had never before been touched by her that way.

Her mother closed her eyes, smiled her child-smile again and sighed a sigh of pleasure. Lorraine kissed her eyelids. She could feel tiny bits of moisture on them. Her mother's skin was so soft. She could remember the smell of breast milk on her mother's skin.

A stack of Bibles rested on the table. Lorraine placed them on the chair. Elvira's eyes followed her the way a baby's eyes follow its mother. She watched the Bibles being placed on the floor. She smiled at Lorraine again.

Later, after she had awakened, Lorraine wheeled Elvira into the recreation room. A group of people seated in wheel-chairs were laughing at a man on TV. Elvira watched atten-tively, then suddenly laughed quietly with the rest of the patients. The nurse walked up to them. 'Good to see Elvira today,' she said as she patted Elvira's hand. She seemed not to notice the room ringing with laughter.

'Why are they laughing?' Lorraine asked. 'That's the President.'

'It's the aphasia,' the nurse screamed above the mounting laughter. 'Their brain is like a lie detector. They don't know. They think it's a clown.'

'And they're supposed to be sick?' Lorraine replied as she joined in the laughter.

'. . . and though in other mortal sympathies and symbolizings, this same hue is made the emblem of many touching, noble things – the innocence of brides, the benignity of age . . .'

*

Through the grill of the confessional, she could see the priest's vestments, the gold and snow white of the Risen Christ. The white lit up the priest's washed-out flesh, giving it a sensuousness that was out of place, unsettling, bold.

'Father,' Lorraine whispered in the confessional when she was fifteen, 'can I ask a question?'

'Go ahead, my child,' the priest said.

'Father, why do we pray for the Jews?'

'We pray so that they might know that the Messiah has come.'

'But they invented the Messiah. They should know if he came or not.'

'What are you saying, child?'

'Well, we're reading *The Diary of Anne Frank* in class and I just wondered if Anne Frank went to heaven?'

'What's your name, child?'

'Lorraine, Father.'

'Lorraine, it is not our concern whether Jews do or do not go to heaven. That's up to God. Our concern is with their conversion.'

'But Father, wasn't Jesus a Jew and . . .'

'For your penance, say five "Hail Marys" and six "Our Fathers" along with one "Apostles' Creed." In fact, my child, say the "Apostles' Creed" along with me right now.'

'But Father, I didn't come to confess, I just wanted to ask . . .'

'Let us pray, Lorraine.'

She tried to see through the dark grill. See the face of the man who would not answer her question. But all that she saw was the searing white of his vestments, the white of his large hand resting on the side of his face, his ear against the grill. She remembered seeing him walk the halls. He was the new priest everyone had a crush on. The young priest who caused all the old ladies to giggle when he passed, the one the girls imagined met the prettiest nun in the school deep in the shadows of the evening after Vespers. The one all the girls flashed their frilly white knickers at whenever he came for Catechism.

'I believe in God, the Father Almighty, Creator of heaven and earth . . .'

Who was this triune male god? Why was it always so necessary to believe all the time? Why couldn't he show himself and save everyone the trouble? Life was hard enough. What kind of game was this god playing anyway who could not trust humans, supposedly the crown of creation, with just a little bit of knowledge?

Why wouldn't this priest answer her question?

The ironwork on the grill of the confessional seemed to dissolve, and there instead were thousands, millions of her ancestors herded off slave ships named *Jesus*, baptized as their feet, unsteady from weeks at sea, touched the ground. The giant cross, the white man's cross, overshadowed their very existence. As it had hers.

'. . . I believe in Jesus Christ, His only begotten son, born of the Virgin Mary, who died for our sins, and on the third day he rose, and who will come again to judge the living and the dead. I believe in the Holy Ghost, the Holy Catholic Church, the communion of saints, the forgiveness of sin, the resurrection of the body, and the life of the world to come, Amen.'

'. . . though among the Red Men in America the giving of the white belt of wampum was the deepest pledge of honor;

though in many climes whiteness typifies the majesty of Justice in the ermine of the Judge, and contributes to the daily state of kings and queens drawn by milk-white steeds; . . .'

There were the long days and nights of caring for her mother, of lying awake listening at night, of hiring and firing the nurses who came and went. Yes, she had to admit to herself, there were times when she regretted her mother surviving the operation, regretted it not only for her own sake, but for her mother's. For everything her mother had worked for, everything that she was, had been destroyed. Destroyed by life itself, with all the capriciousness of an ignorant child.

But she pitied the brothers and sisters of the Tabernacle. Sometimes after her mother had been put to bed, they would sit around the kitchen table, thin-lipped over cups of coffee, everything clean and immaculate the way it had always been, and talk about the past, fearful of the future. She loved them all, loved these old black people, her mother's people. There was something touching about them, in the twilight of their lives, cast out into the darkness of uncertainty.

Once, she said in an effort to cheer them up: 'Hey, maybe this is a test, Mama's just checking out her theory of Radiant Energy, you know how she is.' Brother William, dressed in his ever-present crisp white shirt, recoiled in horror. 'Test! She didn't need a test! She always believed! She never doubted!' Then he stood up and led the group into prayer.

Lorraine did not pray. She could not. There was no use. These people, her mother's congregation, these Christians, would wander around like lost sheep until another shepherd came along to direct them to the Promised Land.

She looked in on her mother then. Elvira was propped up in bed watching a videotape of the President at a news conference. Elvira loved the Presidential press conferences, especially when the Chief Executive thrust his finger out to take another question. Then Elvira would convulse with laughter. A beautiful, free, young girl's laugh.

And always, after the tape had run several times, and she was tired, she would say the only word she could say: 'lake.'

If it wasn't too late, Mrs Robertson would be called to drive them to the lakefront. Devoted Mrs Robertson dressed in her white church 'nurse' uniform, always ready to serve her minister.

They took Elvira down to the edge of the water and sat her on a rock because she loved being up high. She clapped as the waves rolled to the shore.

'Sometimes,' Mrs Robertson would say in her quiet voice, 'you have to ask the Lord just what His plan is. That's what I've been doin'. I don't have the answer, but there is an answer why this happened to your mama. Lord, she could give the most fiery sermons. A female Martin Luther King. She preached so strong that I really believed she could heal the sick through the power of God if she'd put her mind to it. She had that in her. But now . . .'

And then her voice would trail off, lost in some memory that Lorraine could not share. She could not know that Lorraine preferred her mother now. She was free, and a lot more fun.

'Mrs Robertson, Mama can see everything now. There's no yesterday or tomorrow for her. This thing that happened to her brain, it was like she saw the star pointed to Bethlehem, and she followed it. I believe that she understands that she saw that star. She's not confused, Mrs Robertson. She prefers things this way.'

'But she can't even read the Bible anymore,' was all that Mrs Robertson could reply.

Elvira slid off the rock and into the sand. A small boy was making a sandcastle at her feet. He was an albino, his white hair rippled in the gentle breeze. Elvira watched him carefully, as carefully as she watched her Presidential videos. His pale, white hands shaped turrets and battlements. His features were a bleached out African mask, beautiful in its concentration, its stillness.

Elvira joined him in making the drawbridge, then in creating a moat which he filled with the water from his pail.

When the boy was finished, Elvira added a few more touches. Lorraine could see her mother inside the tiny castle, lost in the royal dreams of her childhood.

She worked hard but was clumsy. She knocked a battlement down. The little boy cried. Elvira cried with him, but quickly dried her tears. The smile was always there.

Lorraine helped rebuild it. The albino child scrutinized it with a critical eye. He pronounced it alright. 'Now you've got your castle, Mama,' Lorraine said. Elvira clapped her hands.

Lorraine sat with her on the rock as the sun set and the weather grew cold. Elvira did not want to leave. Mrs Robertson, exhausted from her day's work, fell asleep in the car. When the sun was almost gone, the tide came up and washed the castle away. Elvira crushed what remained.

'. . . white is specially employed in the celebration of the Passion of Our Lord; though in the Vision of St John, white robes are given to the redeemed . . .'

'Look,' Dr Turner said as his nurse prepared the anaesthetic, 'there's nothing wrong with Negroes going on safari. The white man doesn't want us to have any fun. Not his kind of fun. See that elephant,' he said pointing to the mounted head, 'I bagged that elephant, that antelope. Yes, these are my trophies. I don't mess around. I've been to Kenya, I was in the Congo before all that mess started, Rhodesia, all over. Everything's just like America, if you can pay for it. First thing you've got to do is forget all that Black Power stuff. That will get you nowhere. We are not Africans. We are American Negroes. Everywhere, everywhere except here, sees us as Americans first. They all see the American part, and it's fine with me. You young people put too much emphasis on this 'blackness' anyway. It's not realistic. Now, do I look black? Look at my skin. Do you look black? I'm a doctor and I'm telling you there is no such thing as a black person. Or a white one for that matter. Lie back and the nurse'll get you ready.'

Lorraine did not move. Outside the elevated train rattled the building. It shook the metal table with the thin white cloth on it. For a moment she thought the rattle was the wrath of God. God come to condemn her to hell for what she was about to do.

This was not sneaking out after curfew, or cheating on an exam, or smoking in the toilet at school. All of her life she had been taught that black babies were precious. She had grown up with girls who had given birth at fifteen, young enough to still play jump-rope in the school yard, their pregnant bellies flopping out from beneath their sweaters. One woman in the neighborhood was regarded as a heroine because she had died giving birth. A black woman never killed a child. Now she was about to.

Lana had offered to come along, not telling her that the same thing had happened to her. By the same man. But Lorraine decided to make the trip alone. After all, she had made her decision alone. She did not tell Winston. She did not tell him that her mother had noticed that her appetite had increased. Or the fact that she could no longer go to church, either of them. He did not know about the long nights she spent holding her swelling belly, talking to the child they had made, apologizing to it, asking its forgiveness.

The day before the abortion she went back to her old highschool to visit the grotto of the Lady of Fatima, the white gown of the virgin folded over the plaster statue's round belly.

That day a group of novices were visiting the school. They congregated like giggling swans on the school lawn, playing tag in the wind with their new white veils. They still had the giggle of young girls, and the look of young girls, too.

Lorraine joined them, blinded by their stiff, white linen, caught up in their cries of joy, their innocence, their virginity, their freedom in certainty. They were baby Brides of Christ, their lives sealed and delivered.

She could never join them now, not even in her dreams. She knew too much. She felt too much.

The nurse eased her down on the table and placed her feet in the stirrups. Her knees looked funny propped up under-neath the white sheet. They looked like old women's knees, seen from the vantage point of a rocking chair on a hot summer's day in Mississippi. The Mississippi that for her had never existed. Her knees consoled her.

Lorraine closed her eyes and breathed deeply into the cloth saturated with ammonia which was put on her face. In the reception area, Dinah Washington was playing on the radio. There was a portrait there, too, of the 'Queen of the Blues,' swathed in white mink with a tiara of white diamonds on her head.

When the scraping out of her womb was over, she saw a

small pan covered in a white cloth sitting on the table. She wanted to drink it, gulp her baby back down inside of her.

'. . . and the four and twenty elders stand clothed in white before the great white stone, and the Holy One that sitteth there white like wool; yet for all these accumulated associations, with whatever is sweet, and honorable, and sublime, there yet lurks an elusive something in the innermost idea of this hue, which strikes more of panic to the soul than that redness which affrights in blood . . .'

The doctor took his glasses off as Lorraine entered his office. He resembled one of those doctors on doctor soaps who indicate bad news with the twitch of an eyebrow, a gesture to the forehead.

'Miss Williams, would you like a cigarette?' he asked in a perfect doctor-soap voice.

'What, am I facing a firing squad?' she replied, and he laughed the way she needed him to.

'I'm going to give it to you straight, no chaser. Your mother had a stroke on the table. We didn't notice until we got her back in Recovery. It's pretty serious. It's left her aphasic.'

The doctor showed her charts, diagrams, statistics. Her mother would have to learn everything all over again. Part of her brain had been erased. And there was always a possibility that she would have another heart attack.

Once again, Lorraine saw Elvira outside the door of the Tabernacle, the church that her mother built with her hands and her spirit, arguing eloquently over a passage in the Bible. Her powerful voice seemed to come from the heavens themselves, her mind sharp and full of Scripture. Now that sharp mind was gone forever.

All too soon the house was full of the business of dying.

Elvira had always been so pragmatic about death. Once, when Lorraine was a girl, her mother thrust her face up to the mirror and said: 'See that. That's going to be gone some day. You're goin' to die, child, and when you do this will disintegrate, get swallowed up like it never was. The grass will grow over your grave and the world will keep on goin'. And that's the way it is. Nobody's goin' to escape that fact, that's why deep down inside, we're all the same. We all goin' to catch that train.'

For that reason her mother enjoyed the Ash Wednesday service at Mass because of its reminder of mortality. She would go with Lorraine up to the somber altar and kneel before the purple-clad priest as he said, smearing the white ash on her forehead: 'Remember, man, that thou art dust, and unto dust thou shalt return.'

And then one day, her mother was dead. It was a simple dying. She merely opened her eyes, sighed, and closed them again. Its simplicity was almost comical. Then before she could even think about it, Lorraine was staring down at her wrapped in a white gown, her head surrounded by the white satin of the coffin, just like the dead boy she had seen in her childhood.

Lorraine kissed her lips, and sang a song in her ear. She sang the blues, and she thought she could see her mother's face crease into a smile. It made her laugh. Her laughter almost caused a scandal.

Lorraine returned to the house alone. She sat in the dark until a freak snowstorm started. The snow blew against the window, shook the trees still heavy with leaves, rattled the screen door which had not yet been taken down.

In the swirling snow, she could see once again the woman who had lived next door when she was a child in the house her father had visited for one last time. The woman was Muddy Waters' lover and she shook out her white, silk sheets every morning in the backyard, and laughed her great white-toothed smile as she did it. And the music of her laughter.

When the blizzard blew out the lights, she found Oswald's letters. Letters from years back, letters written recently, letters from Greece, and Holland, Belgium, France, and England. Letters written to her mother in response to letters from her.

Lorraine lit the white candles her mother always kept for emergencies and read each one.

Lorraine etched the cities in her heart and buried the letters with her mother. They belonged to her. She would visit every city until she found him. He would return the face she could not see, return it to her in a blinding white light of recognition, of benediction.

He would take his hands and trace them on the empty plain that was her face.

Oswald, her father, would rescue her from this half-life of hanging by her teeth.

diaspora

Amsterdam

Lorraine crawled to a window and bent over the side. Through her drunken haze she thought she saw her father strolling alongside the canal, staring at his reflection in the murky water. But it was another black man.

She had spent three days standing in the Dam Square, the centre of town. If he was in Amsterdam, as the postmark of one of the letters indicated, then he would pass through the Square. Everyone in Amsterdam eventually did. But after three days he had not come. By then she needed a drink.

'April is the cruellest month' she recited to herself as she dry-heaved. The raw spring air slapped her in the face and almost knocked her down. She immediately made up her mind that she had spent long enough in this town. It was time to move on.

The man she was watching below was a junkie. He sat on a bench, nodding off. His cap threatened to fall into the canal. She was fascinated at how he managed to catch it just before it tumbled in the canal, just the way the junkies in New York always managed not to fall over as they stood at strange angles.

Birds landed at the man's feet, picking at the ground around them. The steeple of the Westerkirk, just across the canal, was reflected in the water like an accusing finger.

With the exception of his abundant locks, Bernard Reynolds Abercrombie looked exactly the same as he had the day they sneaked away from the sit-in at university to see *Hair*. He had indeed starred in *Hair* and come to Europe, joining all the *Hair* refugees who found what they believed to be their true home.

He had the same intense, devilish expression, the same slight curve of the neck that gave the promise of an intimacy that was never quite achieved. He walked with the same mixture of goose-step and duck waddle that he had perfected as a ruse to exempt him from the Army. He fell back on it from time to time whenever he was stoned. He had been in Europe now for over fifteen years. And since the walk looked more or less permanent, Lorraine assumed that he must have been stoned for a good deal of his time abroad.

She crawled back to the space in his apartment where she had been sleeping and cuddled up with his doll collection. Bernard's entire flat was crammed with black dolls, what he called his 'Negrophilia' collection. She chose the 'Aunt Jemima' doll to sleep with. It reminded her of Bernard's Aunt Grace who raised him. The doll's body caved in slightly when Lorraine rested her head on it just as Aunt Grace's body seemed to cave in when Bernard announced to her on the hottest day of the year that he was moving to Europe.

The Bessie Smith record played and played as Lorraine tried to sleep. She saw her parents in her sleep. She saw her father in Amsterdam, standing in a field of tulips, calling her name and singing the blues.

When she managed to open her eyes again, Bernard danced his strange walk. 'Your theme song, girlfriend: "Nobody knows my name, nobody knows what I've done," ' he sang along with Bessie. 'And they better not,' he cackled, 'you and me spent our whole lives makin' sure they don't know.' Lorraine nodded her head as she peered into an empty glass beside her. It had the smell of last night's wine.

At the bottom of the amber glass she could see herself once again standing in the car park at the Schipol, peering inside each auto that passed looking for Bernard. She watched the planes take off overhead, the people streaming out of the airport, everything seeming to have its purpose. It was there that she wondered whether she had made a grave mistake coming to Europe. After all, there was no guarantee that she would find Oswald.

And even if she did, what would she do? What would she say?

She had thrown the number of the young black oil executive she'd met on the plane in the rubbish can. Besides, he had gone off with the pretty, young Dutch oil expert. The woman had promised him a sumptuous Indonesian meal, and a tour of Royal Dutch Shell. He was going off with the girl, he assured Lorraine, 'for the brothers back home. Knowledge, sis.' She regretted him leaving. She had desperately wanted to make love to him. She felt that being with a black man from home would give her some sort of anchor on her journey through Europe, the heart of darkness.

Then suddenly, when she thought she could not stand around waiting in the busy airport any longer, a bright red auto on what appeared to be its last legs rattled up. Inside sat Bernard, a brightly colored parrot perched on his shoulder, surrounded by a multi-racial group of young people. Above the din of the bird and the multi-racial contingent, she could hear Bernard's unmistakable Southside-of-Chicago tones

tinged with every place he had ever lived. 'Hey, baby, welcome to Amsterdam, the crossroads of Europe!' he yelled.

Lorraine took the Aunt Jemima doll and held it close. She
expected it to smell of home-made pancakes, of grits and
biscuits, fresh ham, and country eggs. Because she needed it
to. After all, why else did this doll exist except to comfort
Bernard, to give him the sense that in this alien land he had
not lost himself.

He had, during his years in Europe, collected every black
image he could lay his hands on. Crammed in his tiny flat
were posters advertising soap held aloft by coal black angels;
penny banks whose entrances were the gaping mouths of
bug-eyed black slaves; banjo-strumming, bare-footed minstrels
supporting Watteau-inspired lampshades; delicately colored
postcards depicting watermelon-eating children cavorting in
a primaeval South that never existed; sloe-eyed mulatto girls
in white dresses dreaming under big moons with the words
of tropical drinks written across them; thieving black men
outrunning baying hounds in the swamp with the name of
some dog food inscribed down the bark of the trees; fat,
jolly, black women advertising pancake flour; they all rested
majestically, far away from their place of origin, in Bernard's
flat in Amsterdam, overlooking a canal.

'I thought your old man was dead.' Bernard's voice rang
through the room. Light from dying candles lit the dawn-
splattered walls. The room began to spin. Then suddenly
everything turned white. Lorraine was convinced she was
going to be sick again.

She did not know how much later, but when she opened
her eyes, she imagined the sea to be rushing into Bernard's
flat. But it was only Bernard holding a cup of water to her

face. 'If your father is here, there's one place he would definitely be. I'll take you there like the old folks say: "in the
sweet bye-and-bye." '

Lorraine was much too hung-over to argue. As her vision
slowly returned, she could see other people in the room.
Three naked people, a man and two women, were entwined
around one another on Bernard's bed. Another man sat in
the corner staring at her. He was also completely naked. 'Are
you alright?' he asked her in a thick Dutch accent. She
nodded as she searched for the rest of her clothes. She had
somehow managed to undress and put on a pair of Bernard's
huge Mississippi mule-train overalls.

She found her clothes beneath a pile of dolls and staggered
to another part of the room concealed from the rest by a
worn piece of kente cloth stretched across its width. A small
mirror hung on the opposite wall. Lorraine walked over to
it, running her hand along its surface. She only saw Bernard
reflected in it, busy in the kitchen.

'Remember this one?' he yelled. He was playing Bessie
Smith. 'Back Water Blues.' Again.

'I know Bessie wrote it, but I like the way Dinah sings it,'
Lorraine called out.

'You never were a purist,' Bernard said as he stuck his head
around the door, a pan of Moluccan rice in his hand. 'You
never was, "Sweet Lorraine," you just never was. That's niggers for you,' Bernard laughed.

'Excuse me,' the man in the corner interjected, the one
who had been staring at her, 'but why do you constantly
address yourselves as "niggers"?' He had dressed himself by
now.

'Cause we know how to say it pretty, muthafucka, so don't
you try it,' Bernard replied as he served the tea. But suddenly,

Bernard caught himself, as if something had settled in his throat. He looked up to the ceiling, his eyes moist. 'There are birds on the roof,' he said softly. 'They've built a nest. I don't bother them. They raise their babies up there. I don't bother them.' He was quiet for a long time after that. Then he said: 'If your daddy's here, I know where to find him.'

It was then that Lorraine saw what Bernard had always taken great pains to conceal: the tragedy that hovered just below the surface, an unspeakable sadness. If only she could touch him, heal him. She had tried with Winston and failed. With Bernard, too, once, when they were young. In those days he revealed himself more. In those days she revealed herself more. Now there was nothing to reveal. She was being guided.

Now she could understand the meaning of the words from the Bible her mother would sometimes mutter in her sleep. They often came back to her when she didn't know what she was doing. The words of Moses at the Burning Bush:

'Who shall I say has sent me?' Moses asked.

The Burning Bush replied: '*He* Who Is has sent thee.'

'Know who's here?' Bernard shouted, suddenly back again to himself, 'Black Joe Smith. Blackest nigger in the world, remember him? Used to call him "Midnight," and "The Batman," 'cause he wore them black clothes and black shades all the time. Used to say that brother invented Black Power. Remember when they made him 1-A and shipped his ass off to Vietnam after that sit-in we had? Remember when we thought he was MIA? Hey, he wasn't MIA, he was AWOL. Made his way out of the 'Nam to Amsterdam. Don't ask me how. Got here in 1969 and ain't left yet. Got a Surinamese wife and a couple of kids. Been in school here since 1969, workin' on his doctorate or some shit. Playin' the blues and recitin' poetry all over the country. Still wear black. Still crazy. Still Black Joe Smith. He'd know if your daddy was here.'

A shaft of sunlight, a Rembrandt shaft of light, broke through the room. A light full of shadows, it fell on the rows of dolls placed on the mantle, the posters hung carefully on the walls, the family photos scattered in an artfully casual way, the bric-a-brac of life in exile. It splashed on the four Dutch people still asleep. All, with the exception of one, had strong Dutch faces, like the faces of the farmers in Van Gogh's *The Potato Eaters*. They seemed just as oblivious to themselves as their ancestors must have been as they sat eating in the presence of the great gaze.

'I have to go find a hotel,' Lorraine said as she picked up the Aunt Jemima doll, gently punching its soft stomach. 'You stay here! You got to be here for me to take you where you got to go. You got to see Black Joe before you go!' Bernard yelled.

The parrot flapped its wings as if to underscore the demand. It cocked its head in a quizzical pose and squawked 'Power to the people! Power to the people! Right On! Right On! Power to the people!'

That made the four naked people stir. Lorraine recognized them as the trio who accompanied Bernard to the airport. She had been introduced to them, just before a giant spliff was shoved in her mouth. The brown-skinned woman sat up first. She stretched her slim body, her tiny breasts dancing on her ribcage. She scratched her long, black hair, looked at Lorraine and said, 'Hi. I'm Maria. I hope you remember me.'

Of course she did. In the ride back from the airport, Maria had spoken the most. Her voice had a clipped quality with a touch of an American accent, acquired during a year spent in New York. Her mother was from the Moluccas, the island group off Indonesia. Her father Dutch. 'The Dutch don't know what to make of us Moluccans,' she had laughed as they sped into Amsterdam. 'They think all we do is hold up trains. We are not like the Indonesians, you know. We don't walk and talk softly. Moluccan women aren't pretty little dolls. We are black-skinned like you and Bernard. Warriors. When we came here after the War, the Dutch finally had to admit they were racists. And gradually, so many things came forward in the Dutch character.'

She dressed quickly, pulling on a flaming red dress that barely covered her slender brown thighs. But her large dark eyes were wary, like the eyes of a fugitive. Like the eyes of a jungle fighter.

'Are you alright, Lorraine?' she whispered. 'Because sometimes Bernard has quite strong dope. He prides himself on it, I think.' Lorraine nodded. Maria's voice inspired a kind of reverence, there was something small and quiet about it that made Lorraine quiet, waiting to hear the next thing she had to say. 'I heard what Bernard said,' she continued. 'Don't stay with him. You'll be stoned all the time and tripping over pretty little boys and girls. It's what the English call an infant school up here sometimes. No. You can stay with me.'

'Don't listen to that jealous heifer!' Bernard said, as he sprang to his feet, pretending to box Maria about the ears, causing the parrot to flap its wings wildly, depositing a flurry of feathers on the collection of black dolls stacked underneath his cage. 'She's just going to make you into a revolutionary, Lorraine. Watch that bitch.'

'That's the best thing that could happen,' Maria countered. 'I think that Black American women complain too much about their men. I think they live too much in a romantic notion that owes more to a fourteenth-century troubadour strumming a mandolin beneath some damsel's window in Provence, than to any reality today. Black women should look to themselves. That's why I'm taking Lorraine away with me.'

The sun had retreated behind the dingy Dutch clouds as Lorraine, Maria, and Bernard dragged Lorraine's trolley down the cobble-stoned streets back to Maria's flat. 'You know what the Dutch call people who don't pay their fare,' Bernard announced as loudly as he could as they boarded a tram, ' "black tickets." I've been a "black ticket" here for years.' And then he roared so loudly that everyone turned around. 'Now that I have your attention,' he said to an elderly woman who quickly turned her head away, 'I just want to talk to you all about the great Bessie Smith, "Empress of the Blues." '

The passengers were absolutely motionless, as if they were hearing nothing. 'The Dutch are like the English, they can act like nothin's happenin' when everything in the world is happenin',' he said. The tram made a quick turn that knocked Bernard off his feet. He fell in the lap of a small girl who giggled and pushed him away.

'Do you know when I first came here, the little kids didn't giggle at me. They ran away. They said I was "Schwartze Pete," the little black man who helps Santa Claus out. You know how he does that, Lorraine. That little black mutha takes all the bad kids down to Spain to pick oranges and turn black in the hot sun. That is the worst thing that can happen to a Dutch child. Turnin' black. You know, some of these folks don't want to speak Dutch no more 'cause they don't want to be confused with the Afrikaners. Those Boers are their cousins. They want you to forget that, but I don't.'

He stopped again in the way he had done earlier in his apartment, that slow dreaming way as if he were listening to something far away. 'Crazy, ain't it? I hate them, but I love them, too. They gave me my space. I became a person here, Lorraine.'

And then he sank back into his seat, his face as immobile as the face of one of his dolls. Maria put her arm around him. 'Yeah. Black Joe Smith. Black Joe Smith would know if your daddy was here,' he said once again. 'He goes to the Anne Frank House a lot. Go there. He'll tell you. He passed through, Lorraine, on his way West, But he made friends with a white boy at the "Antilles Club." The boy comes there once a week. Ask him.'

Her dreams that night were filled with fields, barren cotton fields, brown and scorched. She walked the fields in the blazing sun. Small, dead animals littered the ground. There was a woman hanging from a tree, her hair on fire, her face blank and featureless.

Her mother and father were dancing in a whirlwind, Elvira in a great white gown filled with stars, Oswald in an African robe which swirled around his body and revealed his thin, dark, vulnerable legs.

They danced and danced. When she ran up and tried to join them, there was no room for her.

Five American tourists shoved past her in the Anne Frank House waving their pre-paid tickets in the air. The first thing they wanted to see was Shelley Winters' Oscar which stood in a glass case in one of the rooms. They spent more time looking at that than at anything else.

Lorraine went immediately up the narrow staircase to the Secret Annexe. She felt dizzy as she climbed, and angry at the tourists who tramped through the tiny space, amazed, as tourists are always amazed, at how small the real thing always turns out to be.

In Anne's tiny space, in the room with the faded photos of movie stars and the view of the Prinzengracht, and the Westerkirk beyond, Lorraine saw Joe Smith. He hadn't changed, except that his face was more lined, and his once generous mouth now a tight, tiny sliver that seemed as if it had never smiled.

She saw the needle tracks on his arms straight away. He barely looked at her. 'Your daddy's been through here,' he said: 'Gone to Paris. Spent a long time listenin' to me talkin' about the 'Nam. About how I used to dream about comin' back to the "world" and then I couldn't come back at all. That inability to come back; I knew that wasn't how a man was supposed to conduct himself.

'I told him about livin' underground for months, and stayin' stoned, and how the language of the 'Nam was the language of the ghetto. Everybody talked it, even the rednecks with their Confederate flag-wavin' asses, they spoke like us, too. Then I had to come back and do this man-thing because a woman back home expected me to be John Wayne and she didn't even know. Your daddy had to go to Paris. Said he needed himself some correct fried chicken.'

That was it.

She watched him climb down the narrow staircase, and out along the same canal that Anne Frank once gazed at, dreaming of freedom.

Brussels and the Dordogne

Maria invited Lorraine to holiday with her, then afterwards she would drive her on to Paris. They were going camping. Lorraine had never been camping before. The thought scared her. Camping reminded her of the film *Deliverance*. She always expected some sort of evil to emerge from the woods.

She fortified herself with some of Bernard's hash, a few shots of vodka, then adjusted herself among the camping gear in the back seat of Maria's boyfriend's Peugeot. As she looked back at Amsterdam, Maria asked over the noisy engine, 'Do you think Bernard will ever return to America?'

Before Lorraine could answer, Peter patted her leg. There was something in the way he did it. Lorraine was grateful for the interruption. She didn't have an answer to the question anyway.

Peter was a dentist as well as a budding tennis champion. He looked like the boys who were always voted 'best looking' in her highschool days with their soft, brown eyes, pencil-thin moustaches, soft, chocolate brown skin, and slightly haughty gaze.

He told her, as they sat once in a 'brown café' smoking hash, that his Moluccan parents lived outside Amsterdam in a nondescript suburb filled with poor immigrants crammed into soulless tower blocks in the flight-path of international jets. She liked his seriousness and his laughing eyes. He was clearly in love with Maria. She was much too intense and in pain to be in love with anyone. Lorraine thought she might show him a thing or two, maybe show them both, at the same time. They weren't going to spend all night cooking hot-dogs over a camp-fire.

They were asked for identification at the border. Maria politely asked the policeman in perfect Dutch if it was because they were black. She cursed him all the way to Brussels.

They had coffee in the Grande Place, the great square which Victor Hugo called the most beautiful in the world. The golden fronts of the guildhalls overlooking the plaza, sparkled with rain. Suddenly, Lorraine heard the unmistakable twang of the Midwest emanating from another table. A woman in a T-shirt and shorts was talking to herself while poring over a map. Her legs were crossed, her mottled flesh seemed to spread out all over the chair. On closer inspection, Lorraine could see that the woman was black. Her pale green eyes were like an eagle's. Her grayish blonde hair hung in damp curls over her forehead. She coughed incessantly as she took hungry drags on a French cigarette.

The woman suddenly looked up to the sky as if she were about to pray. But instead she began a version of Bessie Smith's 'Backwater Blues.' 'Not that song again,' Lorraine thought. The woman's voice almost sounded like Bessie's, too, the same long moan, the same girlish hint of pleasure and mischief. It caused a table of French tourists to stop talking and listen to her. The entire square seemed to listen to her. She sang from her heart. And when she sang, the Grande Place with its soaring balconies, cafés, and powerful statues, seemed to come into being. Conjured by the voice of an elderly black woman far from home.

When she finished, there was a scattering of applause. The woman bowed with a great flourish, then turned to Lorraine, winked, and said something to her in French. The woman then stared at Lorraine. 'You American?' she asked in a deep voice, ignoring Maria.

She soon joined them. Her name was Shirley. She had come to Europe after the War to entertain the black troops. She had travelled all over Europe singing for black men. Then after her tour of duty was over she decided to stay on. She married an Italian count who managed to have a heart attack on their wedding night. This left her with a modest fortune. She spent it all on a French boy who turned out to have a wife tucked away in some sleepy village in the South. She then returned to work, singing in cabarets all over Europe. She made more money than her late husband had left her. Josephine Baker had been her friend. She had known Eartha Kitt then, Orson Welles, Cocteau, Aly Khan and Rita Hayworth. She dined with the Duke and Duchess of Windsor, and was best friends with Sidney, their Jamaican valet. She cooked greens for Louis Armstrong and Duke Ellington.

Shirley had lived a hundred lifetimes and now she wanted to make one more stop before she returned to the Detroit she had not seen in over forty years.

Without pausing for breath she said to Lorraine: 'I want to see the Congo Museum, the place where they have the dead statues.'

Maria and Peter stayed in town while Lorraine and Shirley journeyed out the next morning to the museum. 'Shit, don't it make you scared when something's this clean?' Shirley roared as they stood on the platform of the pristine metro.

She wore a colourful Hawaiian dress with a red flower in her hair which made her resemble some South Seas Queen Mother. She carried an ancient Louis Vuitton suitcase. 'Mine was made at the same time they created that big trunk for Leopold Stokowski. I knew him, too, when he was married to Gloria Vanderbilt.' Mock gold 'Arabian Nights' slippers adorned her feet.

She had persuaded Lorraine the night before over several Kir Royales, to wear a lovely red silk scarf around her neck to offset drab, sensible Brussels.

An African woman with bright eyes, and carrying her child on her back was also standing on the platform. Shirley walked up to her and began immediately to speak in French. The woman laughed and giggled, nodding her head excitedly. She rode in the same car with them, talking as animatedly as Shirley did. Her baby played peek-a-boo with Lorraine. As the woman alighted, she gave Shirley and Lorraine a big kiss. She then waved and laughed from the platform.

'What did you say to her?' Lorraine asked.

'Honey,' Shirley roared, 'we talked about men. White, black, yellow, or polka-dot, they all the same.'

A tiny train took them out to the countryside where the museum was located. 'Yes, I played the Cotton Club,' Shirley continued, 'knew Lena Horne then. She was a shy thing. Had a face like the Virgin Mary with mischief on her mind. See, I was one of the ones they called "high yellow clean and holy." Yes, of course I loved it. Who wouldn't love it when you had a glamorous job in the middle of the Depression! But I quit 'cause I knew there was something more in the world. Then War broke out. Lord, I remember that day. I had a boyfriend up in Harlem, a man black as the ace of spades. I ain't never in my life seen a man that black before or since. They called him "Blue" 'cause baby, he was blue-black. Skin was all messed up because he had smallpox as a child and the boss wouldn't let him have any care. This was during the First World War, you see. Blue wasn't nothin' but a baby, but he just knew in his heart how he was bein' treated and why. He had his revenge on that peckerwood, but that's another story.

'So Blue and me are reading the papers in bed, when the news come over the radio about Pearl Harbor. And Blue jump straight up out that bed like a cat on fire and started yelling "The colored folks done bombed Pearl Harbor! The colored folks done bombed Pearl Harbor!" He was as happy as if some of them from 125th Street had done it. That man was so happy that somebody was whippin' the white man that he started learning Japanese. Child, you should have seen this Alabama nigger black as coal speaking Japanese like he was born in Tokyo. I was scared for him, though. Real scared. People didn't like it. They called him a Jap lover. The FBI was sniffin' around. He had a heart thing, so they couldn't draft him. But they wanted him to do something, you better believe it. I joined the service to kind of take the heat off him. People startin' sayin' "You know, Blue must be alright 'cause his woman has joined up." Like that. He died of a heart attack when they dropped that A-bomb on Nagasaki. Somebody said his last words were "the white man won again." '

The tiny train chugged through the countryside, parting the great forest as it went along. Shirley sang to herself again, her lovely voice ringing through the car. An Australian couple clapped their hands softly in time to the music. An elderly Englishman smiled in his sleep. Shirley patted Lorraine's knee gently. 'Don't you worry, child,' she said softly, 'Shirley's here.'

After they paid their admission to the museum, Shirley marched Lorraine into the first room she saw. It was decorated with the armoury of conquest. A statue of Leopold, King of the Belgians, who as master of the Congo treated the colony as his personal domain, dominated the room. 'I had a lover once from Zaire,' Shirley whispered as if she were in church. 'He said that what the Belgians did to his country they had never seen in Africa before. It was Leopold's thang, his playground. My boyfriend had to get out after 1960. Too much killing. That man never had a good night's sleep. Not one night. Don't tell me about Africa!'

There were documents in the room. Shirley studied each one carefully, then wrote in a tiny notebook which she carried in her Vuitton suitcase. She took dozens of photos of the statues, most of them of imperious white men in mutton chop sideburns with cruel eyes.

Shirley paused before they entered the next room, as if she needed to take a deep breath. Lorraine could feel Shirley's body tremble. Shirley's eyes, formerly so full of fire, now misted over as they walked through the gallery where masks, statues, and instruments were displayed in antiseptic white cases, enclosed behind glass, and bathed in a cold, white light. Earth brown, ochre the colour of dried blood, green like the great hills Lorraine imagined Africa to have, all the colors of life vibrated in the dim room as if they were giving off one last signal.

Lorraine understood why Shirley wanted to come. This was not a museum, but a morgue, a morgue of the spirit. Everything of spirit that had been in the statues was now gone. The knowledge of this reverberated through every pore of Lorraine's being. It was as if something seared before her eyes taking a layer away from them. She was almost dizzy with the sudden sight. The dying power of the room made her tremble.

Shirley did not take notes here, nor did she take pictures. Instead, she made little sketches in her notebook of surprising accuracy. 'I have to put my hand to this,' she said. 'A photo could never capture what I see now.' She worked quietly and quickly.

Lorraine could hear the artisans in this room, those who had created the work as a force of society, not as something to decorate a cold room in a cold, damp country. Their cries were locked in the wood, and they had been stolen away, as she had been stolen away to exist on a foreign shore, unsure of the way back. Like them, she was behind cold, white glass. Lorraine began to cry.

'Wipe your eyes, child. Don't worry. They took all the ju-ju out,' Shirley said. 'When they crossed that ocean sea, no matter how they crossed it, they left the ju-ju behind. Those statues died. My man from Zaire told me that. He said: "Go see all the dead statues. All of them. In Europe and America. Africa, too. Go see. Then you'll understand something." So I have. And yes, now I see. Crossing the water did take all the life out. Took it all away. I had to see for myself before I went back.'

And with a great sigh, Shirley pushed them outside to the lovely park, urging her to take great gulps of air in order to choke back their rage, their tears. In the dim Belgian light, Lorraine could see the tiny veins on Shirley's nose, the drooping lids over the once sparkling eyes, the skin stretched and sagging, the death mask beneath the smile. Lorraine put her arms around her. Shirley then collapsed sobbing like a child.

A group of boys, their pale hair gleaming in the light, ran toward them out of the forest beyond. They were like a flock of wild birds, boys with long limbs and loud voices, crashing into one another until they stopped abruptly before them.

'Bonjour, mes enfants,' Shirley suddenly chirped.

The boys gave her a cheery 'Bonjour, madame.' They turned their attention to Lorraine who did not speak. 'Madame,' they said.

'Hello,' Lorraine replied.

'Anglaise? Americaine? Canadienne?' they asked eagerly.

'Americaine,' Shirley interjected, suddenly back to life, 'and don't you forget it. New York City. So nice they named it twice.'

The word 'New York' danced through the boys like a grass fire. They gathered around Lorraine and Shirley, staring at them in awe and reverence. Shirley laughed as Lorraine attempted to respond to their rapid French. Suddenly, a stern-faced, thin man came trudging through the woods. The boys quickly dispersed, the word 'New York' ringing through the trees.

The man touched his hat and bowed. He said something to Shirley in a low, gravely voice. Suddenly, all the incandescence that had gone out of her in the museum returned. She was luminous. She was once again the beautiful girl in the chorus of the Cotton Club half a century ago, an ivory-skinned Jean Harlow watched hungrily by some crown prince of a minor principality. The crown prince who dreamed of long nights of primitive passion tucked away in a suite at the Hotel Teresa on 125th Street.

'What did he say?' Lorraine asked after he had left.

'Lorraine, he said I was more beautiful than anything they got in that building. I don't care what the goddamn French say about the Belgians. They got taste.'

Later Shirley said: 'Now, ask me why I did what I just did, draggin' us out there.'

'OK, why . . .' Lorraine began, but Shirley put her scented finger on Lorraine's lips.

'Because, Lorraine, when I sit in my sister's living room back in Detroit, rocking back in my rocking-chair looking at *The Price is Right*, trying to act like I belong, I want to have these pictures. Do you understand now?'

It was already dark when they arrived back in Brussels. The great square was illuminated. A strolling violinist was walking among the tables. Two young African men made eyes at them as they passed. They were beautifully dressed, their gold wristwatches gleaming from the light of the candles on their table. One of the men motioned to them. 'Sapeurs,' Shirley laughed, 'rich boys with money to burn. Clothes are their country, their religion. They spend $10,000 on an outfit, and change two, three times an evening. Their girlfriends hold their clothes-bags all night. All those brothers do is style and profile. Rich Africa in Europe having big fun.'

Lorraine listened, but she couldn't help the sudden deep craving clawing at her insides for the one with the slanted eyes, the tribal scars, and head-to-toe Armani. But Shirley dragged her away. 'Players, honey, livin' on their daddy's money. You don't want to be nobody's fourth wife.'

It was then that Lorraine's eyes began to burn slightly, as if they were adjusting to a new kind of light. For some reason the burning in her eyes made her eat more food than she intended. Shirley ate, too, continuously ordering wine. Story after story tumbled from her lips as they sat in the plaza, surrounded by the gilded statues of a dying culture.

Shirley talked, but Lorraine did not listen. She watched instead the still lovely mouth that seemed on the verge of tears. Like the mouth of a young child, crumpled and trembling, unsure of what to do.

When Lorraine returned to the hotel room, Maria and Peter were already asleep. Maria had left a note: 'Eight tomorrow,' in her careless script. Lorraine slowly undressed, the only light the light from the square. Her eyes hurt her. She could barely see. But when she looked out of the window at the plaza from their over-priced hotel, she could see Shirley still sitting there, dreaming of Detroit and the end of the world.

Peter's auto, a quick buy on the outskirts of Amsterdam before they left, made its torturous way through the hills of the Dordogne. Lorraine had never been driven up a mountain before. She cowered in the back seat as they ascended, a true child of the flatlands, astounded at how easily the Act of Contrition came to her lips.

In the front seat, Peter and Maria were completely oblivious to her fear. When Maria caught sight of Lorraine in the mirror, she burst out laughing. 'You should see yourself! Look at your face, Lorraine. Peter, turn the mirror around so that Lorraine can see her face.'

Lorraine pulled her head up and looked into the mirror. 'Look at you,' Maria taunted.

In the mirror, Lorraine saw the winding road disappear behind them. She saw the sunlight dancing in the trees, the sky, and the face of the child she once was, wide-eyed and blinking at the great world her mother showed her at the edge of the lake when she was a little girl.

Then she would stand with her mother, gazing at the great body of water that never seemed to end, and dream of the wide expanse beyond, and the places she knew in her child's heart that her mother longed to see, too. Longed to see if fate had not confined her to the prison of her sex and race.

When they arrived at the camp, a sun-tanned, bouncy grandmother-type in shorts and top ran out to greet them. When she closed the gate behind them, she took off the shorts. Lorraine looked around. This was a nudists' camp.

Resigned, she stretched out beside the pool and closed her eyes. She had discarded her bathing suit because she felt more self-conscious with her clothes on than off.

When she opened her eyes, she saw a limp, pale penis hanging above her. It was attached to a very tall, thin, slightly balding man with glasses. A little black boy hid behind him.

'Hello!' the man boomed in sing-song English. 'My son is very shy. He has never seen another black person before. We live in a part of Holland that does not have very many black people. I'm not sure, but I don't think we have any black people at all there. So my son is curious. He wants to know what you sound like.'

Lorraine sat up and tried to cover herself. She forgot where she was. When she realized it, she shrugged and thrusting her hand forward, in her broadest American accent said: 'Hi.' The little boy jumped.

'Does he speak English?' she asked.

'Oh yes,' the man replied, 'just as well as I do. The other day we sat down to study together and I asked him "Henrik, where is your nose?" Watch, please.'

He turned to the boy who had partially emerged from behind him. 'Henrik, where is your nose?' The boy pointed to his foot. 'Wonderful. And your mouth, Henrik?' Henrik touched his crown. 'Your ears, Henrik . . .'

'Right, you better stop there,' Lorraine said. 'I'm scared you're going to ask him where his face is.'

'We don't believe in discouraging our children,' the man replied sternly.

Henrik moved closer to Lorraine, so close that they were almost touching one another. He took her arm and held it next to hers. He looked from his arm back to hers. He rubbed his own flesh and then tentatively rubbed hers. When he saw that nothing came off, he smiled.

'We adopted Henrik, of course. He's from the Pacific. His parents were very poor. I worked there and so I thought, Why not? Why not bring this little black boy back with me to Holland. He is very loved. We love him. Everyone does. But I think it is true that he is lonely for his own kind.'

'Young Henrik speaks very good Dutch. First class,' Maria said as they ate supper that night to the sound of the boy's excited chatter at the camp-fire next to theirs. Henrik and his family were eating on the other side of the hedge. Once in a while, Henrik would glance over.

'They must be professional people. I think the man is an art historian or something,' Peter added. 'All he talks about are paintings.'

The night was clear and full of stars. Lorraine sat in the bunkhouse washing her legs. She was much too suburban Chicago to sleep outside. A sick child slept in one of the bunks, her breath a dull rattle in her chest. Her mother came in and out with a thermos of soup, her long breasts flapping with each step. She smiled at Lorraine as if she were the nurse. There were many times that Lorraine thought the woman would speak to her. But she only managed a weak smile, her eyes full of fear.

In the moonlight, Lorraine could see Henrik pacing up and down. He was walking in the open area, playing alone with the volley-ball nets. Sometimes he would look back at the bunkhouse, just standing with the wide-legged stance of a child. Lorraine watched him for a long time, then went outside.

The moon illumined his skin. It made the blue-black of it look silvery, enchanted. She knew that somewhere a council of elders mourned his loss. He had the face of an elder, the face of a man who had seen many things. His dark eyes were full of things he could not express. All of it locked in the body of a child.

She walked beside him without saying a word. Soon he took her hand and walked close to her. She knelt and stroked his face in the moonlight. He smiled his old man's smile. He stroked her face. She kissed him, and for a moment, he pulled back, just as he had done earlier. But then he came closer. And for a moment, she could see it. Her face. A glimpse reflected in his eyes. She reached for it, but it quickly vanished among the other things in his eyes. Among the cool palms of his Pacific atoll, the ocean that had been his life, and the flesh of his mother aching with longing for him.

Paris

There was no such thing as the 'real Paris,' Lorraine decided. Paris was the dream city, it existed in the dreams of everyone who dreamed about it. Her dream was to stand in the Tuileries and see her father singing the blues.

She wore dark glasses now because her eyes showed her what she had not seen for a long time: her face, her face in all its different ages, the face that had become distorted, lost in an attempt to live a life that had never been her own.

That face came unbidden, now, reflected on every surface she gazed in, everything she glimpsed.

Even here, in a hotel room in the Latin Quarter, she could see her emerging face, the half-formed eye staring in her mother's womb, her face listening to the muted love-making of her parents.

Oswald's letter from Paris mentioned the Tuileries, the gardens behind the Louvre. Lorraine went there every day. She stood near the men from Senegal and Mali, their skin the colour of tree bark, those men who sold wooden birds and snakeskin handbags, their faces impassive, their voices monotone and blank.

She drank every night until she staggered back to the

hotel, lost among the students who sang songs in the narrow streets just as they had been sung for centuries. She would sit half-naked on the balcony overlooking the winding street. Nothing mattered any more. The Arab grocer sat on his stoop below, surrounded by lemons, and mango fruit, staring up at her open legs.

She went again to the gardens for the last time. Her money was running out. She would have to leave Paris soon if she was ever going on to London, the place where her father had last written from. She bought a snakeskin handbag as a souvenir. Just as she handed over the money, she saw Winston coming toward her.

At first she thought it was a trick of her new eyesight. Winston. In Paris. She had not seen or heard from him in years. She did not respond until she heard his voice. It was the same, familiar and warm, as if he had expected her to be there all the time.

Lorraine removed her glasses. She could see, with her new eyes, not only the way he was, but the way he had been. That beauty was still there, so mesmerizing, so immediate, that there were times when she thought him her twin, the very mirror of her being.

She could only nod when he asked her to meet him at Père Lachaise the next day.

That night she went down and drank with the Arab grocer. He told her about his land back in Algeria, how he had fought for the French and when they lost, he had come to Paris, barely surviving that night in the sixties when over a hundred Arab men lost their lives in a racist frenzy. His son, who was born in France, wanted to live in Algeria. He hated the 'fromages.' But there was nowhere for him to go. In

France, he was nothing. In Algeria, he was the son of a traitor. He had no choice but to roam.

Lorraine went with him to the back of his shop. She wanted to hold the man, hold life before she met Winston tomorrow in a place of death. The grocer had a good smell, like herbs. She allowed him to undress her, and as he did what he needed to do, what she needed him to do, she watched her face in the broken glass which hung over the photo of his farm in hills far away.

She met Winston at the place in the cemetery where the communards had been shot over a century ago. He did not greet her when he walked up to her. He did not speak to her for a long time as they walked in the city of the dead. And when he did speak, he acted as if he were a tourist guide, pointing out the graves of the famous dead.

He took her hand and rubbed the crotch of the reclining statue on top of the grave of a young communard. It had been rubbed many times before and was now as shiny as the foot of a plaster saint. 'Baby,' Winston suddenly whispered. He took her hand and put it inside his jacket for warmth.

He guided her through the necropolis, up the gently rolling hills, through the thick foliage fertilized by the bones of the dead. He held her hand as if they were on a picnic, one of their famous outings in highschool when he would borrow his father's Lincoln with the power steering and air-conditioning, and take her far away, deep into the areas where whites still hunted blacks for sport. Far away past the smoke stacks of the South end of the city, and the dirty Calumet River that was the dividing line.

Out to the high, deep prairie, the place of tall grass that black people feared because it hid so much. He would pick wild flowers for her and put them in her arms, great bunches of them, their drooping heads staining her clothes. They would make love in the tall grass with their eyes open. Open in order to see their faces reflected in one another's eyes.

With him in that place, all of her love and fear of God, her deep questioning, all evaporated next to him as they counted the clouds that passed by. 'I'm not going to be a tragedy,' he said so often to her when they went there. 'I'm not going to be a tragedy like a lot of brothers are.' He made this promise to her so many times and in so many ways. And he said it again to her now, in the city of the dead, thousands of miles away and many years gone.

'I'm not going to be a tragedy. And neither will you.'

A tall, strong-looking black woman blew a whistle indicating closing time. She had a big, open face full of mischief and happy secrets. She winked at them as she stomped big-footed along the path. She looked back at them and winked again as she disappeared among the tall monuments.

Suddenly, Lorraine took Winston in her arms. His body felt frail, broken, so delicate that if she squeezed him he might shatter into a million pieces. Instead, she rested his hands on her arms. It was the same way she touched her father when he hugged her as a little girl.

Winston's face was always so smooth, as smooth as a woman. Indeed, there was something still soft about him. Something that she could hold in her hand and cherish. Something that had finally broken through out of all the years of male reserve to come wet and trembling to her. She could be the stronger and wiser now. She could take him by the hand and lead him through the dense meadow, and place him on his back in the tall grass, undress him, love him.

She took him back to her hotel and to her bed in the

early evening. She held him tight and rocked him like a baby so that he cried as the night grew darker. She made love to him as he would have once made love to her. She felt herself grow stronger with each time. She kissed his soft face and said the things to him that he had said to her on hot dormitory evenings when her roommates were away. On hot dormitory evenings when they made love to the sound of the blues on a cheap record player bought on Maxwell Street from a Mississippi master with shattered ambitions.

In the morning he told her he lived with an African woman, a strong, sweet woman who had a hair salon in Barbes and was older than him. She wanted a baby, and he wanted to roam. She allowed that, and next month he was to be a father.

He took her to his woman who was small and wise. Her hands smelled of peanut oil as she read Lorraine's palm. She said something in Twi to Winston. 'Go to London,' he repeated to Lorraine, 'your daddy is there.'

Lorraine's eyes were like lasers now. She knew she was in Paris, in the Gare du Nord on her way to the Channel, but yet this was not a railway station in Paris. This was somewhere else. She could see them all now: all of those who had died, those who missed her, those she missed. So many gone, now crowded into this station, travelling with her on the journey south to cross the water.

And when she looked among them, she saw herself, her own face. The face she had when she set off from Chicago years ago and into her life. The face she could not see was now here. She kissed the greasy glass of the railway car. She kissed it. No one said a word.

She turned to wave goodbye to Winston. Goodbye to her only love . . . But he was gone.

St James Park, London

Lorraine took her usual place on the park bench. She had been coming here for several months. She trusted in her newly found sight, and whenever she saw a vision, or had 'second sight' which seemed now to come to her more frequently (she didn't quite admit all of this to herself, she just had visual 'feelings' she'd tell herself), then she would act immediately. She didn't doubt any more.

During one of her 'feelings' she had seen a park bench. And so she promptly went to a park in the centre of town, which she thought was a good idea. She sat from day to day, in all kinds of weather.

She managed to rent a small attic room from a witch. The witch was the daughter of a lord and had run away to Spain where she had discovered the Goddess and women.

Lorraine allowed her to make love to her for a while. Their lovemaking was soothing. It did not feel alien in this alien land. But the witch had become possessive.

The witch beat a Celtic drum every evening at sundown when Lorraine wanted to listen to Dinah Washington. Then one day the witch no longer spoke to her, and Lorraine found herself alone once more.

It had been impossible to work legally in London, so she sold everything she had and became a bag lady. It betrayed every stricture by which she had been raised. This felt just fine.

She thought often of the black people she met in Europe, the exiles who looked westward with regret. She was not like them.

She had no country at all.

One day the witch invited her to a ceremony. They were

celebrating the Goddess. There was going to be wine and food. Lorraine did not eat often, so she went. Everyone there was naked, so she took off her clothes, too.

She was conscious of her ageing flesh. She had lived too long. Life itself had become a chore.

But she would live long enough to see Oswald Williams again. If she had to sit on a park bench for the rest of her life.

Then one day a black swan came dancing up the path. Behind it, playing a harmonica, was an old black man, his step as spritely as a boy's. She had to squint to make him out. But she knew who he was.

This was the man she had been waiting for. But she had discovered her face all on her own. She would tell him. She would tell him that she had found what he had taken.

He stopped not far from her. The sense of quiet around him was astonishing. It was as if he sucked up all the air around him, and made it peaceful. She could sit beside him forever, father or no father.

Then he spoke to her: 'Nice day, huh?'

She almost fell off the bench. The first words her father had spoken to her in person since she'd been a little girl!

She leaned over to speak to him. She leaned over to let him see her face, let him trace with his eyes his own immortality in the broken-down person of his daughter. Then they would mourn together the woman who had never really lived. His wife. Her mother. Herself.

But he could not see her. Oswald Williams was blind. Blind to all she had gone through, blind to what she had been, blind to who she was now. What had it all been for? He touched her hand, then eased himself up. The black swan flapped out of the water and followed him down the road.

Lorraine watched her father disappear. Watched him swallowed up in the people. Then she knew.

She had not been searching for him at all.

Athens
Now

Lorraine twists the engagement ring her Bajan fiancé has planted hastily in her palm at Gatwick Airport. Her head is pounding like a brass band from the ouzo. The ragga girls are acting up.

She pulls her big hat down further on her head to shield her face from the sun. Athens is a hell-hole in the summer, she thinks. Old ladies drop dead from the heat in Athens in the summer. Old ladies like me.

When she returns to London, she and her husband-to-be will have to find a house, probably some respectable little bungalow in South London. She'll decorate it like her childhood home. Funny, she laughs to herself, how much you become like your mama when you get older.

She suddenly realizes that it is too quiet. The ragga girls have disappeared.

She walks through the winding streets, tucked away from the intense light. She can hear her feet on the cobble-stones. Feel her feet moving.

Everyone back in London is delighted. 'It's about time you settled,' they tell her. They keep asking if she'll have children. All black women must have children. It's an African thing, an ancestral thing.

Lorraine cannot imagine herself standing at a school gate

at fifty-six with a ten-year-old waving frantically at her. It's much too late for all that.

After she marries, she's decided, she will join a weight watcher's club, learn to drive, go back to Barbados with him, her future husband the Head Teacher. She will walk beside him and be his wife because . . .

Anyway, she is tired of moving.

Suddenly, she hears the bells again. She knows that sound. She turns the corner into a small square. Yes, it's the same church. And there she is. The Black Virgin again. 'La Retour.' She walks in, and finds the icon. She stands before it for a long time.

Then, gathering her courage, she peers into the darkness, peers into the ancient face. Another vision. Herself. Old. She is walking across a flat plain. Not in America. She is walking unattached, walking back to the place where she had come before. The lost home. Long ago.

She can hear the blues again. Someone is singing again. It doesn't matter where the sound comes from. She no longer has to know. She no longer has to know anything.

She takes off her engagement ring and places it carefully at the base of the icon. She takes all of her identification and puts it there, too.

Lorraine takes a deep breath and walks back out into the square. It is almost dusk. Soon the people will come out again. The shops will be opening. The ragga girls will be looking for her.

She looks back in the direction she came. Then she turns, plants her feet firmly on the road, and walks away. In the opposite direction.

Founded in 1986, Serpent's Tail publishes the
innovative and the challenging.

If you would like to receive a catalogue of our current
publications please write to:

FREEPOST
Serpent's Tail
4 Blackstock Mews
LONDON N4 2BR

(No stamp necessary if your letter is posted in the
United Kingdom.)